What the critics are saying...

"*Crime Tells: Cady's Cowboy* is a wonderfully written story full of suspense and sizzling sex...The story is fast paced with quite a few twists and turns that will keep you interested and reading. Cady and Kix have a chemistry not only in their sexual encounters but also in the investigation... As with *Lyric's Cop*, the first in the series, the secondary characters are also interesting and will keep you on the edge of your seat, waiting for their stories. Enjoy *Cady's Cowboy*...it's a great read with strong characters, steamy sex, and a thrilling storyline." ~ *Trang, eCata Romance*

"If you're craving something a little on the wild side and love sexy cowboys, then *CADY'S COWBOY* is the book for you." ~ *Sinclair Reid, Romance Reviews Today*

"*Cady's Cowboy* is the second installment in the *Crime Tell* series. *Ms. Jory Strong* has penned a page-turner suspense with so many plot twists and turns that I can guarantee you won't figure out the ending. This is a true "who done it" that just happens to have one of the hottest cowboys a little filly would ever want to meet. So, if you like strong quick thinking heroines and hot cowboys, with voices to melt hearts, not to mention various pieces of undergarments, this is a definite buy for you." ~ *Raashema, Euro-Reviews*

"*Crime Tells: Cady's Cowboy* demonstrates why I like *Ms. Strong's* books. Cady and Kix were unique characters, and their personalities never felt forced or exactly the same as characters from previous books. The sex seemed just as laidback as Kix, yet was still hot." ~ *Dani Jacquel, Just Erotic Romance Reviews*

"Once again, *Jory Strong* creates a strong plot that enhances the attraction between the compelling protagonists...The eroticism of this story is based in a powerful and enduring love from the first time Cady and Kix make love until the end. This second *Crime Tells* story is an excellent follow-up to *Lyric's Cop* and features many of the same characters, and some new faces too. *Ms. Strong* continually surprises readers with her inventive plots, thrilling romances, and believable characters. Don't miss this story!" ~ *Sarah W, The Romance Studio*

"*Crime Tells: Cady's Cowboy* is a steamy, seductive novel that laces intrigue, suspense, and romance into an exciting web of mystery. The relationship between Cady and Kix is as complex as it is erotic... The interaction between her characters has this reviewer anxious to discover what she plans for the third installment of *Crime Tells*. This is definitely a series worth reading!" ~ *Chelyjo, Coffee Time Romance*

"*Cady's Cowboy* offers a compelling mix of hot romance and a thrilling plot. I'm looking forward to the coming books in the Crime Tells series." ~ *Stephie, Cupid's Library Reviews*

JORY STRONG

Cady's

Crime Tells COWBOY

ELLORA'S CAVE
ROMANTICA PUBLISHING

An Ellora's Cave Romantica Publication

www.ellorascave.com

Cady's Cowboy

ISBN # 1419952897
ALL RIGHTS RESERVED.
Cady's Cowboy Copyright© 2005 Jory Strong
Edited by: Sue-Ellen Gower
Cover art by: Syneca

Electronic book Publication: May, 2005
Trade paperback Publication: November, 2005

Excerpt from *Calista's Men* Copyright © Jory Strong, 2005

Warning:

The following material contains graphic sexual content meant for mature readers. *Cady's Cowboy* has been rated *E-rotic* by a minimum of three independent reviewers.

Ellora's Cave Publishing offers three levels of Romantica™ reading entertainment: S (S-ensuous), E (E-rotic), and X (X-treme).

S-*ensuous* love scenes are explicit and leave nothing to the imagination.

E-*rotic* love scenes are explicit, leave nothing to the imagination, and are high in volume per the overall word count. In addition, some E-rated titles might contain fantasy material that some readers find objectionable, such as bondage, submission, same sex encounters, forced seductions, etc. E-rated titles are the most graphic titles we carry; it is common, for instance, for an author to use words such as "fucking", "cock", "pussy", etc., within their work of literature.

X-*treme* titles differ from E-rated titles only in plot premise and storyline execution. Unlike E-rated titles, stories designated with the letter X tend to contain controversial subject matter not for the faint of heart.

Also by Jory Strong:

Cady's Cowboy

Crime Tells

Trademarks Acknowledgement

The author acknowledges the trademarked status and trademark owners of the following wordmarks mentioned in this work of fiction:

Starbucks: Starbucks U.S. Brands
Chevy: General Motors Corporation
Harley: Harley-Davidson Motor Company
Jeep: DaimlerChrysler
Winchester: Olin Corporation
Gulfstream: Gulfstream Aerospace Corporation
Jack Daniels: Jack Daniel's Properties, Inc.
Volkswagon: Volkswagen Aktiengesellschaft
Jockey: Jockey International, Inc.

Chapter One

Cady Montgomery shuffled the cards and prepared to deal. If they'd timed this right, then their grandfather, Bulldog Montgomery, would call them into his office just about the time someone was raking in the all-or-nothing jackpot.

Her eyes moved from the pile of chips in the middle of the table to the office door, then back to her two sisters. It usually didn't take Bulldog very long to sum up a potential case and decide whether he wanted to take it on.

Until he'd semi-retired, Bulldog was one of the most sought after detectives in the gambling business. Casinos all over the country hired him when they thought they were being ripped off, either by gamblers or their own employees.

He still worked those cases occasionally, but when he did, he usually took at least one of his grandchildren with him. These days, Bulldog's focus was on spending more time with his family. That's why he'd started Crime Tells — *tell* being a gambling term for the clues or hints that players or dealers unknowingly give about the cards they control.

Now Bulldog took on a wide variety of cases, anything that grabbed his interest or seemed like something his grandchildren would enjoy working on. Besides Cady and her sisters, Erin and Lyric, Crime Tells also employed their cousins, Shane, Braden and Cole. And there were plenty of other Montgomerys and Maguires waiting in the wings for their chance to work for Bulldog.

Cady grinned. Could it get any better than this? She got to work with her family and also build a clientele as a professional pet photographer. That was another great thing about working for Bulldog—he was flexible.

She dealt the cards. "Anybody see who went in?"

Erin pushed some of her blonde hair back from her face. "No. I was in the darkroom when Bulldog paged."

Lyric reached for her cards, the movement dropping a curtain of black curls onto the table. "Alex Martin."

"Valley Training Center. Two-time Olympic medal winner in dressage. That Alex Martin?" Cady asked.

Lyric nodded. "You know him?"

"I've done some photo shoots over at his barn."

Erin wrinkled her nose. "Lucky you."

"Let's sweeten the pot," Cady said before she picked up her cards.

"Winner goes down to Starbucks and gets us some mochas?" Lyric's voice was hopeful.

Cady laughed. As much as she and her sisters were different, they were also very much alike. "No. Winner gets to be lead on the case."

Erin laughed. "You're still sore from the stakeout."

"Yeah." Cady's body ached just thinking about all the hours she'd spent sitting in the car on Erin's last case. "You guys in?"

"I'm in," Lyric said.

Erin nodded. "Me, too."

Their timing was perfect. Just as Cady laid down the winning hand, their grandfather opened his office door. "We've got a case here. Who's lead?"

Cady pushed the wild mass of brown curls back from her face. "I am."

Bulldog nodded. "Take it then."

They moved into the office and headed for their usual seats, though Cady had to relocate a dappled dachshund from her favorite chair to the cedar bed behind Bulldog's desk before she could sit down. Thanks to one of Lyric's pet detective cases, there were now *a lot* of miniature dachshunds in the Montgomery and Maguire families.

As soon as the introductions were made, Cady directed her attention to Alex. "Even though you've already talked to Bulldog about the case, we'd like to hear it straight from you."

Alex nodded. "I can't provide very many details, but I can give you an overview. A friend of mine is a trainer over at Bay Downs. Last week she had five horses test positive for cocaine. All five of them raced on the same day and won. The racing officials took her license away, but Adrienne is innocent."

He cut a quick glance over at their grandfather. "Because of your connections to the gambling industry, I came here for help. I want you to find out who drugged the horses and why, and gather enough evidence so that Adrienne can get her license back."

Cady's eyebrows drew together. "Will the racing officials be investigating this? Five in one day is pretty suspicious, and I'd guess that cocaine is not the usual drug of choice."

Alex shrugged. "They may make a stab at investigating, but they're not required to prove Adrienne is innocent, not when the evidence says she's guilty. The tracks operate under the Trainer Insurer Rule, something that was put into effect to keep the racing game 'clean'. Basically it means that a trainer is absolutely responsible for their horses."

"So Adrienne stays suspended if she can't prove her innocence?"

"Yes."

"What does Adrienne say, besides not guilty?"

"She swears that she has no idea who would want to ruin her."

"We'll need to talk to her."

"Adrienne is expecting you." Alex pulled a business card out of his pocket and quickly scribbled on the back before handing it to Cady. He shifted in his seat and for the first time, he seemed uncomfortable. "There's a slight complication that I need to warn you about."

Cady groaned inwardly. One thing she'd learned since she began working at Crime Tells, there was always more to every story. "Might as well lay it on the table. What's the complication?"

"There's someone else investigating the matter on Adrienne's behalf."

"A private investigator?"

"No. He's not a PI, but he is in law enforcement—a sheriff to be exact, from some podunk town in Texas." Alex's face puckered as though he'd bitten into a particularly sour lemon.

Cady's eyebrows drew together. "This picture is not coming together for me, Alex. Why would a sheriff from some 'podunk' town in Texas be up here investigating something like a trainer's license being taken away?"

Alex shifted again, this time looking less sophisticated and more than a little worried. "Apparently Kix is one of Adrienne's old boyfriends."

"Has the sheriff made any progress on the case?"

Alex's expression darkened. "Not that I'm aware of, though he says not to worry, that he'll handle it."

"So you've actually met him?"

"Yes."

Curiosity prompted Cady to say, "And?"

Alex stiffened. "What I think of that cowboy sheriff isn't important. What is important is getting Adrienne's name cleared and her license back. Racing is her livelihood and her life."

* * * * *

Kix Branaman sprawled on the antique couch, watching the ultrasophisticated Adrienne blush like a schoolgirl as she finished her conversation with Alex Martin. Love—it made fools of the best of them. Kix shook his head, glad his hide was as tough as an old range bull's and he'd never suffered from that particular affliction.

Adrienne gently set the phone down. "They took the case. One of Bulldog Montgomery's granddaughters is on her way here."

Kix's eyebrows shot up. "A woman PI? Maybe you should set Alex straight and tell him there's nothing going on between us so he doesn't waste his money."

Adrienne's frown was severe. "Your chauvinism is showing and it's not very flattering."

Kix put a hand over his heart. "You're cutting me with your words, Addy. Take them back or I won't be able to go on."

Adrienne shook her head. "I think Alex is right. It makes sense to have someone local helping you."

Kix snorted. "I know more about detecting than most PIs will ever know. And don't tell me that Alex is doing this for my benefit. Soon as you introduced me, he acted like a stallion whose mare roamed a little too close to some other stud's pasture."

A fresh blush washed over Adrienne's face but she didn't deny his charge. Kix grinned. Hell, he and Adrienne had gone out a couple of times. Why not? They'd known each other since they were kids. But there wasn't any chemistry, no matter how much their families would have liked there to be, and how much easier it would have made things. You didn't grow up in their world without developing a huge amount of cynicism about why people liked you, and what they ultimately wanted from you.

The doorbell sounded and Adrienne rose from her chair. "That must be her now." She shot Kix a look that was part haughty demand and part desperate pleading. "Please behave, Kix."

"Don't you worry, Addy. I'll behave and you'll be back at the racetrack in no time flat."

* * * * *

As Cady rang the bell, all she could think was, *Damn, horseracing has been good to Adrienne McKay.* The house in front of her looked like something right off the glossy pages of *Architectural Digest*. Cady half-expected a maid or butler to open the door. But the woman who did could only be Adrienne. Double damn. Adrienne looked like she'd walked right off the cover of a fashion magazine and next to her, Cady felt like someone who'd been speeding down the highway in a convertible.

Adrienne stepped back and said, "Thanks for being willing to help. You look familiar. Have you been a private detective for long?"

"Not that long. But you might have seen me on the track. I do some professional photography. I've been there a couple of times to do portraits."

Adrienne's face cleared. "You did the portrait of Joe Metzger and Challenger. I saw it when I had dinner at his house. It's beautiful—you really captured Challenger's spirit."

Cady flushed with pleasure. "Thanks."

Adrienne waved Cady in, then led her through several rooms, all elegantly furnished and tastefully decorated. Cady was amazed by the sheer number of Faberge eggs. They were everywhere, some out in the open on jeweled stands, others housed in glass cases—all temptingly beautiful.

They ended up in Adrienne's office and Cady's throat went dry at the sight of the man sitting there. He looked like he'd just stepped out of a "Sexy Cowboys of the West" calendar. Lean, lanky, gorgeous—and unfortunately well aware of his effect on women. The smile he aimed at Cady was lazy, inviting and had her nipples beading up against the thin barrier of her shirt—not to mention her insides turning into a warm, sticky mess.

"Well, darlin', you're just about the best-looking PI I've come across," he drawled as he unfolded himself from the sofa in Adrienne's office.

The photographer in Cady appreciated everything about him, from the tousled sandy-blond hair, the warm chocolate-brown eyes, straight nose and full lips—to the lean, no-fat-allowed body and the jeans that were faded, most notably where they stretched tight over his very noticeable erection.

His chuckle when she got to that area of his body sent fire across Cady's face. She jerked her eyes upward and got treated to a perusal much like the one she'd given him. "Well now, working with some local talent is starting to look mighty fine to me," he murmured.

Adrienne said, "Kix, this is Cady Montgomery. Cady, this is Kix Branaman."

The cowboy stepped forward and took Cady's hand. She prided herself on not melting into a puddle at his feet when the smell of his cologne wrapped around her. Damn! He was a walking pheromone time bomb as far as she was concerned.

Kix figured that just about every drop of blood in his body had gone to his cock. Whoa, but helping Adrienne out had just gotten a whole lot more fun. He was rock-hard and hurting just looking at the woman in front of him. And her scent... Well, he was fantasizing about burying his face against that gorgeous little body and...

Adrienne fought to keep from laughing out loud at Kix. He looked like a barn cat that'd found the cream. Oh, he might make jokes about his hide being as tough as an old range bull's and how love made fools of the best of them, but she knew that was just because he hadn't met the right woman. Until now, maybe? Adrienne sighed. If something good came out of this nightmare... She sat down in a chair, almost forcing Cady to take a spot on the couch.

Kix grinned and sat down on the couch next to Cady. Yes, sir, this little vacation was looking better every second.

"How much did Alex tell you, Cady?" Adrienne asked, getting right to the point.

Cady made herself stop thinking about the male distraction next to her and concentrate on gathering information. "Not very much. He said that you lost your trainer's license after five of your horses tested positive for cocaine in one day."

"Well, unfortunately that's about the whole story. It's every trainer's worst nightmare. I can't be with the horses twenty-four hours a day! Anyone could have slipped those horses the cocaine."

"As a performance enhancer?"

Adrienne nodded. "It would be, but no one in their right mind would use it. Everyone knows it's a drug the track tests for. You don't have to have a criminal mind to figure out that the trick to drugging a horse is to find something new, something that the tests don't pick up yet. That's common knowledge these days—you only have to turn on the news to sports or watch the Olympics!"

"How often are horses drugged?"

Adrienne shrugged. "Occasionally you hear rumors. But let's face it—having a horse that moves fast or is drugged so it doesn't realize how much its body hurts is just one part of the equation. If it breaks out of the starting box poorly, or gets boxed in behind other horses, it could still lose the race. There just aren't any guarantees in horse racing. And then to top it off, any suspicious or high dollar betting is reported to the race officials right away."

"Do you have anyone watching the horses at night?"

"Yes, Don. He's a retired cop. Kix has already talked to him. Don swears he didn't see or hear anyone bothering the horses."

Cady forced her libido down and risked a glance at Kix. "What do you think about the guard?"

Kix gave Cady a smile that made her think of smooth chocolate and how she always licked the bowl clean whenever she made cake. "Well, darlin', I think he might be guilty of sleeping on the job, but that's about it."

She turned her attention back to Adrienne. "When did the horses race?"

"Thursday. And before you ask, I'll tell you the same thing I told Kix. The horses I run are owned by family members, or by me. As far as I know, no one in the family is either mad at me or in trouble financially and hoping to score big by winning at the racetrack."

Cady's eyebrows shot up before she could stop them. It wasn't just Adrienne who was rich. She had to have come from a family with money—lots of money—if they all owned racehorses. "What about fired employees and jealous rivals?"

"No fired employees. Jealous rivals…" She shrugged. "I hadn't thought so."

"This doesn't come across as a random act."

"Believe me, I've been racking my brain. I just can't come up with anyone who hates me this much."

Cady risked a glance at Kix—surprised, and a little unnerved, by his mostly silent presence. Damn! He was distracting. Her nipples were still so tight that they ached, and all she could think of when she looked at him was how she'd like to pretend he was chocolate and eat him up. No wonder Alex was worried about competing with Kix. The man was just plain delicious. She refocused on Adrienne. "How long have you been a trainer at Bay Downs?"

"I started my operation here about a year and a half ago."

"Where were you before that?"

"New Jersey and Florida."

"Why the move?"

Adrienne hesitated before saying, "Alex."

Cady's heart did a little jump, though it would take a monster earthquake—or a game of poker with her sisters—to get her to admit how happy Adrienne's answer made her. "How are your horses running?"

"Overall, I've been happy with them." Adrienne grimaced. "There isn't a lot of big money to be made up here. When I want to run for the big purses I have to ship them down south or back east."

"Santa Anita?"

"Yes, and Del Mar."

"How successful have they been?"

"Well, including the horses I still have an interest in on the east coast, plus the winnings from betting on them, last year they pulled in over five million."

"Not too shoddy."

"It kept the family members off my back." Adrienne's eyes sparkled when she smiled.

Somewhere in the house a door slammed and Adrienne's smile disappeared as footsteps pounded down the hallway toward the office. A moment later a girl-woman stormed in.

She was lean, mean, and jockey-tiny. And while she didn't look like she'd visited the front cover of *Glamour* magazine, the family resemblance between Adrienne and her was obvious.

"Goddammit, Adrienne. Nobody'll put me up. I can't even get on as an exercise rider. Nobody'll touch me! It's like they think what happened to you will rub off on them."

Adrienne's mouth tightened. "We'll talk later, Terry."

"Fuck that, Adrienne! My life is going down the shit-hole because of this mess." She jerked a thumb in Kix's direction. "I thought he was going to get things fixed up. Instead he's sitting here on his ass."

Kix stood and moved in front of the angry girl. "Well, Terry, I figure you've had your say. Now get out."

In response, Terry took a swing at Kix and Cady's heart pulsed with shock, then turned over at the sound of his amused laughter. "That's no way to behave," he said as he deftly dogged the punch and grabbed the girl's arm, twisting so that he had her locked against his body. "We can play this two ways." His drawl faded into a cop voice. "Either you settle on down, or I'll call in a favor and you'll spend the night downtown sorting things out in a cell."

"Let me go!"

"Soon as you decide how you want to play this, Teresa."

"Fuck you, Kix!"

Kix shot a look over at Adrienne. "You mind dialing for me?"

"Kix…"

"No, seems to me that Terry has made her choice. She's old enough to know what she wants."

With a worried expression Adrienne picked up the phone. Terry stopped struggling and Cady could see the moment when the angry girl realized that Kix wasn't bluffing.

"Okay, fine. We can talk later," Terry mumbled, her face sullen.

Kix slowly released her. "Talk if you've got something helpful to say but keep your mouth shut if you're just planning on bitching. Understand?"

Terry's face went ugly and Cady's breath locked in her chest as she waited for another violent scene. Tense silence hung for several seconds before Terry said, "Fuck it. Fuck you," and stormed out of the room, slamming the door behind her.

Adrienne's sigh was shaky as she glanced at Cady and offered an embarrassed smile. "I'm sorry you had to witness that. She's my cousin. Unfortunately she's part of an arrangement I have with my uncle. I get the horses, and her."

"She lives with you?"

Adrienne sighed again. "Yes. Terry lives here and works for me. She's a jockey."

"Is she any good?"

"She's got tremendous talent and most of the time her personality is…less objectionable."

Kix snorted and sat back down on the couch. "That's true if your idea of 'less objectionable' is a rabid ranch dog that's tethered instead of running free. If it was me running the show, I'd load up those horses and Terry and pay the freight to send them back home, 'cause one thing's for sure, you send 'em COD and nobody is going to accept the delivery."

Cady did her best to hide a smile. Adrienne frowned at Kix but Cady thought the other woman was having a hard time maintaining it.

"Is there anything else I can tell you?" Adrienne asked.

"No. I'll give you a call if something comes up. In the meantime, I'll follow up with some people I know and see if there are any rumors floating around at the track."

Adrienne's hand shook just a little bit as her hand settled on a trophy and she traced her fingers down the sleek legs of a galloping horse cast in bronze. "I really appreciate your help. It's like being dropped in the middle of a nightmare and not being able to wake up."

Cady's heart went out to her. "My sisters will also be working the case if needed. Between the three of us, we'll find out who's behind this." She stood and said, "Well, I'd better get going."

Kix stood also. "I'm right with you, darlin'." He moved around the desk and gave Adrienne a hug. "You hang in there, Addy."

Adrienne hugged him back. "Call if you find out anything."

"I'll do that." He winked. "Don't wait up for me."

Cady's heart did a happy dance before she could tell it that Kix was just trying to lighten the mood and *not* implying that he'd be spending time with her. She gave Adrienne a quick smile and headed back toward the front door. Within seconds she felt Kix's presence in the hall.

"Whoa, there," he said and Cady's heart started trotting at the sound of his voice. He caught up to her before she could get through the front door. "What's your hurry, little darlin'? Seems to me that we should figure out how we're going to work together."

Cady stopped but didn't look at him for fear of making a complete fool of herself by drooling. "Maybe we could touch base over the phone," she mumbled.

Kix's low rumble of laughter felt like a warm tongue stroking her clit and Cady's already damp panties grew damper. He was lethal!

As if guessing the direction of her thoughts, he murmured, "Don't worry. I don't bite, not unless I get asked."

Cady closed her eyes briefly and willed herself to get a grip on her hormones. A guy like Kix probably got by on his charm and good looks. Heck, he probably couldn't stop himself—in fact, maybe he wasn't even aware of what he was doing. She risked a peek. Strike that, he was well aware of what he was doing. Taking a deep breath, she said, "Okay, but if we're going to work together, do you think you could tone down the randy ole cowboy routine? I'd like to help Adrienne, but I'd like to keep things professional between us."

Kix's smile was slow and sure. "Anything you say, darlin', any way you want it."

Chapter Two

Cady wasn't sure how she ended up with Kix in her truck, though she had a sneaking suspicion her hormones had overridden her brain. That was a first.

Well, at least she'd managed to prevail when it came to who was driving. That was something, wasn't it? She hadn't gone totally brain-dead when Kix had turned the charm on full blast.

"Well, little darlin', where are we heading?" Kix asked as he flipped through her collection of CDs and selected one.

"Hermosa Ranch. That's where Erin and Cole and I keep our horses."

Kix's eyelids dropped and his mouth quirked up. "You like to ride?"

Heat washed across Cady's face at the images his question evoked. Damn! Did everything out of his mouth have to feed into an erotic fantasy?

"Yes," she answered, knowing it applied to both his question and hers. "Do you ride?"

"Every chance I get."

Cady's knuckles tightened on the steering wheel. *I'll just bet you do.*

Kix chuckled. Hell, he didn't know what it was about Cady, but he couldn't stop himself from teasing her. 'Course, it could be the major hard-on he'd been sporting since he'd first seen her. Damn, those wild curls and that tight little body made him want to fall into bed and ride her from sunup to sundown. And her little speech about "toning down the randy cowboy routine" and keeping things professional was like waving a flag at an excited bull. Goddamn but she was something else.

Cady snuck a look at Kix and relaxed when he seemed to be deep in thought. So far she'd managed to hold her own, but she wasn't sure she could handle being around him for long stretches—not that she hadn't been hit on before, but he was *way* out of her league.

Pulling into the ranch, Cady spotted the real reason she'd decided to stop there first. Miguel Hermosa. Seventy if he was a day, Miguel had practically grown up at Bay Downs—stall cleaner, groom, exercise rider, and finally jockey. He'd lived to ride, but it had eventually chewed him up and spat him out. Like a lot of jockeys, he'd lost his way in the bottle—trying to hold on to a dream that required him to be pounds lighter than his body wanted to be.

Miguel was sitting under the shade of the shoeing area. As soon as Cady slipped out of the truck, he pushed back his hat and said, "Hi there, sweetie. Who've you got riding shotgun today?"

Without turning, Cady could feel the warmth of Kix's body next to hers. She introduced the two men then asked, "Do you still have any friends working at Bay Downs?"

"Nope. All dead or they finally smartened up." He shook his head. "Still got a few who think they're going to strike it rich in the grandstands."

"Professional gamblers?"

Miguel snorted. "More like fools. Hanging out every race day, throwing good money after bad."

Kix laughed and Cady wondered why the sound was powerful enough to melt her insides. She said, "You think they'd be willing to talk to me?"

Miguel stroked the short gray stubble on his cheeks. "Sure, sweetie, not every day a pretty young thing wants to spend some time with them. Red would get a kick out of it. So would Jimmy and Ernie."

"What do they look like?"

"You can't miss 'em. They'll be sitting right down near the rail. Red wears a straw cowboy hat with a red feather sticking out of it. Jimmy the Sweep looks like you'd need a big shoehorn to get him in and out of his chair—man lives to eat and bet the horses. And Ernie is a small guy. Sometimes we call him The Weasel. He's got a face that kind of reminds you of one. But more than that, he's got a way of digging around and picking up information."

"Thanks, Miguel."

"You be careful, sweetie."

Cady couldn't help shooting a sideways glance at Kix. "Always."

Kix laughed softly at the challenge she'd just issued. He couldn't wait to get her underneath him. Hell, he couldn't wait to get her on top of him. He'd give her a no-holds-barred ride that she wouldn't get anywhere else. Damn, but she was driving him crazy.

Truth be told, he hardly had to lift a finger and the women came running. Between being the sheriff and being part of the Branaman clan, he almost had to use the nightstick to beat them off.

There'd been a couple of fillies along the way who'd tried to play hard to get, but Cady was the real deal—a heap of honesty laced together with sensuality. She'd probably be a hellcat in bed — with the right man. And he was planning to be that man.

Kix grinned. She felt the attraction, and he'd bet his favorite truck that her cunt was all slicked up and waiting for him. And her nipples — they'd been as hard as his cock from the moment Adrienne had introduced them. Now he just had to get her to stop dancing out of reach and accept what was going to happen between them.

"Not a bad lead, darlin'. The Weasel sounds like a good man to talk to," Kix said when they were on their way to the racetrack. He couldn't resist the temptation to lean closer and brush the wild curls back from her face.

For a split second she allowed the touch, then color rushed to her face and she jerked away from him. "Do you think you could stay on your side of the truck?"

"I reckon I can try if you really want me to."

Cady risked a glance in his direction and immediately wished she hadn't. He was just…too masculine…too sexy…too adorable…too everything…and definitely too much for her. "Are you sure you're really a sheriff?"

"Yeah, been one for the last five years." He grinned and she was immediately entranced by the sparkle in his eyes and the little dimple next to those kissable lips. His eyebrows moved up and down. "You want me to bring out the handcuffs, or do you want to move right to the nightstick?"

Cady forced her eyes back to the road, though she had a harder time forcing erotic images of being cuffed to the bed out of her mind. Not that she'd ever even come *close* to experiencing that fantasy, but with Kix — whoa, *nix* that. She was *not* going to get involved with him. He was trouble with a capital H for heartbreak.

When they got to Bay Downs, Cady pulled out her camera and made sure she had release forms along with film. Besides being a great cover for investigating, she genuinely loved photography—it was one of many things she had in common with Erin and Lyric.

Kix quirked an eyebrow. "No digital camera?"

"Not on Bulldog's cases. He wants to have negatives."

Kix picked up her camera case and studied the laminated business card glued to the front. "Cady Montgomery, Professional Pet Photography." He grinned. "This for real?"

"Yes." Cady cringed inwardly when she heard the defensiveness in her voice.

"Would have pegged you for a doer instead of a looker."

"What does that mean?"

A slow grin settled on Kix's face. Damn if she wasn't as prickly as a hedgehog. "I'm just surprised you're a picture taker. Way I've always seen it, there are two kinds of people—those that stand around watching life go by and those that take it by the horns and ride it for all it's worth."

Cady frowned at him. "A person *can* be a professional photographer and live life to the fullest, just like a person *can* be good at multiple things. Not everyone"—her eyes conveyed a silent *like you*—"is good at only one thing. I'm also a good PI and a damn fine poker player."

His laugh stroked right over her. "Well darlin', I'm good at a lot of things, too. In fact, I've been known to play a mean game of strip poker, myself. Maybe later we can see who's better—just to set the record straight."

Before she could stop herself, Cady's eyes dropped to the still very noticeable bulge in his jeans. "Pass."

Kix chuckled. "Darlin', at least hesitate for a minute before you slam my ego."

Her eyes moved back up his body until she met his gaze. God, he was hard to resist. She was a sucker for men who had a sense of humor and didn't take themselves so seriously. "I'll bet you weren't even raised on a ranch. You probably grew up in the city watching westerns."

Kix slapped his hand on his chest. "Darlin', you wound me. I was born and raised on the Kicking A Ranch—home of fine horses, fine cattle and mighty fine men."

"Of which you're the exception."

Kix took the opportunity he'd been waiting for and moved in, trapping her against the side of the truck before she could escape. He speared his fingers through the silk of her hair and turned her face up to his, delighting in the way her cheeks flushed with color and her eyes couldn't hide the fact that she wanted this as badly as he did. "Darlin', I can't let that insult to my manhood go unchallenged." He dipped his head and sealed her lips with his own.

Cady melted the moment his mouth covered hers. When his tongue teased her lips open and stroked inside, she felt like someone had poured warm honey into her.

The man could kiss. That didn't surprise Cady in the least—what did was the fact that she not only let him, but couldn't help returning the kiss. She wanted to eat him up.

Kix groaned in response and pulled her even tighter against him, thrusting his tongue in and out in a rhythm that had her cunt clenching and her nipples straining.

Cady shivered and pressed closer. God, he should be banned or jailed—everything about him was sinful and tempting.

He shifted again, burrowing his cock closer to where it wanted to be. Damn, but this attraction had him feeling like a bull rider who got tossed and stomped on right out of the chute. If he didn't get a tighter hold on himself, he was going to end up hog-tied and too sorry-assed in love to care.

They were both breathing hard by the time the kiss ended. Cady somehow managed to move away from him, her eyes once again dropping to the erection that pressed boldly against his faded jeans.

Kix grinned. He was randy as a stud and lighthearted to boot. "You're a mighty fine distraction, little darlin'."

"I do have a name," Cady muttered.

Kix pulled her against his body, tight enough so that his heavy cock pressed against her. She shivered in response. His answering laugh was low and husky as he whispered a kiss along her neck before nuzzling her ear. "Oh, I plan on using your name all right, Cady, just like I plan on hearing you scream mine."

Cady's nipples were so tight that they ached. She closed her eyes against the sensations bombarding her. She was swollen and wet and so needy that she wasn't even sure masturbating would provide any relief. Damn, how had she gotten into this mess?

Kix brushed a kiss against her neck. Damn if touching her hadn't been a big mistake. Sure enough, he could do more than one thing at a time, but walking around with more blood in his cock than in his brain was a damn nuisance. He grinned. But one he was surely going to enjoy dealing with later.

Cady escaped as soon as Kix dropped his arms. Her body felt like it'd go nova if he touched her again. Forcing a stern expression on her face she said, "Adrienne's counting on us to help her...so maybe we should concentrate on that instead of out-of-control hormones."

Goddamn if she wasn't twisting him all around inside. "Lead on, darlin'."

Taking a deep shuddering breath, Cady headed toward the grandstand.

They rounded the corner and came to a stop at the sight of the protest in front of them—well, "protest" might be too strong a word. Three women were sitting down, headphones on, listening to music and playing cards. Two others, one man, one woman, were carrying signs that read "End the Race" and "Stop the Exploitation".

"Reckon they're protesting in shifts? The three sitting down sure look like they're on break."

Cady couldn't resist saying, "That's what I thought, too. I'm glad to see that you can think about something besides sex."

Kix chuckled. "You mean put the big head to use?" He leaned over and brushed his lips against the skin beneath her ear. "Be careful, darlin'. I have a long memory and I'm a believer in seeing justice served—even if it means I've got to mete out the punishment myself."

Cady tried to squelch the erotic images that his threat conjured up—but enough of them got through to cause another round of panty-soaking. At this rate she'd probably end up in the emergency room for dehydration—how embarrassing would that be!

She decided to ignore him. "I'm going to go talk to them."

"You go right ahead, darlin'. They might take me for a rancher and try to skin me alive or maybe club me with those signs. I'll wait here."

Cady snickered. "I thought you said the Kicking A Ranch is famous for fine beef."

His laugh was smooth molasses. "Sure enough is, but I'm no rancher. Seems like I've always worked on the shit-shoveling end. Figure that's why I ended up a sheriff."

She grinned and dared a quick look at Kix. God, how was she going to be able to resist him? His sense of humor alone made her want to wrap her body around his and take the ride of a lifetime.

Cady shook her head and resolutely moved toward the protesters carrying the signs. They didn't seem overly friendly until they spotted the camera bag. "You from the newspaper?" the man asked. He was medium height, brown-haired, with a pencil-thin mustache and eyes that had a habit of darting around like he was afraid he was going to miss some action.

"No. I'm a professional photographer." Cady watched as the man's interest in her faded and his eyes flicked away. They only came back when she asked, "What are you guys protesting?"

The woman looked at the man first. When he didn't answer, she stepped closer and Cady couldn't help but compare her own suntanned skin to the woman's ultra-pale complexion. "Do you know what happens to racehorses when they're washed-up?" the protestor asked.

Cady had a pretty good idea, but decided to play along. "No."

"They end up overseas on somebody's dinner table. Or they end up in dog food. But before they get there, they go to auctions where kill-buyers bid on them by the pound. Then those beautiful horses are crowded into double-decker trailers and taken to the slaughterhouse. They travel from here to Texas without food or water. They can't lie down and they're forced to stand in urine and feces." The woman stopped to take a breath.

"How do you know this is what happens to ex-racehorses?" Cady asked. She didn't doubt that some ex-racehorses probably ended up at the slaughterhouse, but she didn't know what percentage of them did—the information wasn't something the racing community readily shared. For that matter, the topic of surplus horses wasn't something that the equestrian community liked to discuss at all. Cady and Erin had talked about that quite a bit, especially after they'd helped a writer friend by taking pictures of horses being sold by the pound at auction.

The protestor hustled over to where the other three protesters were still on break. There was a green knapsack leaning against the wall of the building. She dug into it and a minute later returned with some literature, thrusting it into Cady's hand. Cady glanced at it long enough to see that it was put out by the Animal Freedom Front. She shivered. *When you sup with the devil, be sure to use a long spoon.* No way would she ever tangle with them like Lyric had.

"Would you guys mind if I snapped a few pictures?"

"Why do you want our pictures?" Thin-mustache sounded suspicious.

"I'm a photographer. Today I'm trying to capture images from the racetrack."

Excitement flared in the woman's eyes. "Are you working on a book—like one of those 'Day in the Life of' books?"

"Well, it's too soon to tell," Cady hedged. "I'll have to see how the pictures turn out."

"What do you say, Danny?" the pale blonde asked her companion.

He thought it over, then shrugged. "Okay."

The woman hurried over to the three sitting protesters. They lifted their earphones and listened to what she had to say. A moment later all five of them were holding signs. Cady started taking pictures. When she was finished, she pulled out the release forms.

The protesters weren't thrilled about signing the forms, but they gave in when she explained that she couldn't use the photos without signed releases. It was true, and it was also one of the things she loved about combining detective work with photography. Having a shot at fame usually tempted people to turn over all kinds of handy information.

By the time Cady got back to where Kix was waiting, the three women protesters had donned headphones and gone back on break. He shook his head. "Nice work, darlin', though I figure I've seen more passionate protestors at a 'Save The Trees' rally."

They paid their admission and pushed through the turnstile.

"Hold on," Cady said, walking over to purchase a race program from a man who looked like he might fall asleep any minute. She fought against breathing in the smell of stale sweat and alcohol as he took her money and handed her a program. "Busy day?"

The man grunted. "Place is dead. Same way it's dead every day. Don't know why I bother showing up."

Cady turned back to Kix. His eyebrows moved upward. "You planning on gambling?"

"I like to bet on the horses," Cady said defensively. Not that she did it very often — mark that, almost never.

Kix shook his head. "It's your money, darlin'. Where to?"

"Don't you have any detecting of your own that you need to do?"

Chapter Three

"Now darlin', you're not trying to get rid of me are you? Won't work if you are. Today I'm all yours."

A quick glance at his face and she bit her tongue. He had innocent down pat. Cady shook her head. "Let's go find Miguel's friends."

"After you, darlin'."

Just as Miguel had predicted, his friends were hanging out in the seats closest to the rail. The feather in Red's cowboy hat bobbed up and down as its owner made a show of tearing up his betting tickets and throwing them in the air.

Jimmy the Sweep was biting into a foot-long hot dog. Ernie the Weasel had his snout in the *Daily Racing Form*.

Cady took a seat next to Red and gave all three men a smile before saying, "Hi, I'm Cady Montgomery and this is Kix Branaman. Miguel Hermosa said we should look you guys up. He said you knew everything there was to know about racing."

Jimmy started cackling. "Got that right." He stuck out a beefy hand. "Jimmy. But my friends call me 'The Sweep'."

"Why the nickname?" Kix asked as he shook the offered hand.

Red started laughing. "'Cause of the way he bets. Man's got no balls, uh excuse the French, Miss Cady. Always bets to show."

Cady laughed. "No offense taken." At the racetrack there were three options — to win, to place, or to show. Betting to show meant that a horse could come in first, second, or third and still be in the money. The few times they'd come to the track, that's the way Erin had bet. Lyric of course always went for complicated combinations that spanned several horses and several races. Cady bet whatever seemed best at the time, though she usually bet to win or to show, instead of splitting the difference and gambling that a horse would "place" by coming in first or second.

The Weasel offered his hand to Cady. "Ernie, my good lady. That's my name." He cast a look at his friends and added, "Others might call me by another name, but in superior company such as yours, I'd prefer to be known as Ernie."

"Ernie it is."

Red took his hat off before offering his hand, first to Cady and then to Kix. "Red's the name."

"Glad to meet you," Cady said.

Red grinned. "If you don't mind, we've got to sort out our bets, then we can talk."

Cady turned her attention to the grandstand. There were more people gathered around the television monitors inside than were out watching the horses race. "There aren't very many people here," she said to Kix.

He shrugged. "Adrienne told me that things were tough. You've got Indian gaming and some card clubs for starters, plus Internet sites and the entire state of Nevada. Kind of hard to compete against all of 'em."

"Who are you betting on?" Red drew Cady's attention back to the three men. He was standing, program in one hand, a fistful of dollar bills in the other.

Cady glanced down at her program. "Which race are we on?"

Jimmy snorted. "Second."

There were ten horses running in the second race. Cady scanned the names, then flashed a smile in Kix's direction as she pulled a couple of dollars out and handed them to Red. "Slick Moves, to show."

Ernie the Weasel hooted. "My good lady, that colt has never run worth a damn. He's fifty-to-one."

Cady looked over at the board displaying the current odds and her smile grew wider as she cut another look in Kix's direction. "Yep, that seems about right, though his odds of making it across the finish line might still be overstated."

Kix laughed and retrieved a five-dollar bill. "I think the lady underestimates the stud. I'll put five on Slick Moves to win."

Ernie shook his head. "You two should hang on to your money. Next race, we'll try and help you out."

The loud speaker announced that the cutoff for betting the second race was only moments away. Red scrambled for the betting windows. A few minutes later he returned with the tickets.

Slick Moves was a liver chestnut that came out of the saddling enclosure prancing and snorting. "Don't get your hopes up," Jimmy the Sweep said. "He'll burn up all his energy before they even get him in the starting gate. Happens every time." He pointed to his *Racing Form* as though the information was there, for all to see.

At the starting gate, Slick Moves was in the number five position. Red shook his head. "You need a miracle with that horse. He's going to have to break well and get to the rail in the lead. Otherwise he'll end up boxed in, with no way of making a winning move."

The bell sounded and the announcer yelled, "And they're off!" From then on it was a second-by-second relay of what was happening on the track.

Slick Moves broke to the rail but was in the middle of the pack at the start of the race. As they rounded the first curve, Cady lost sight of him. But in the backstretch she saw him again and he was making his move.

He'd managed to find an opening and was now closing the gap between himself and the front two runners. Cady stood up and started yelling for him to run.

As the horses hit the home stretch, Slick Move's jockey used his whip and the liver chestnut colt leapt forward, giving it his all. At the wire he managed to edge out the first-place horse by less than a nose.

In her excitement Cady hugged Kix. He grinned and took advantage of the contact, biting down on her earlobe before whispering, "Reckon the odds are getting better for me. Don't you worry, darlin', you won't need a crop to get this stud across the finish line." A jolt of searing heat shot from Cady's earlobe straight to her cunt.

"Jesus," Red said in disgust and for a moment acute embarrassment raced through Cady. But when he made a show of tearing up his betting ticket and throwing the pieces into the air, she realized that his curse was directed at the race's outcome and not at Kix's suggestive comment.

"Behave!" she whispered before disentangling herself from Kix and returning to her seat.

"Hey, hand me a candy bar, will ya," Jimmy said, pointing to a bag at his feet.

Red shook his head but leaned over. "You gotta stop eating and drinking every time you lose. Already takes a shoehorn to get you in your seat."

Jimmy snorted. "Luck's going to change and when it does, I'll go on a diet."

Ernie the Weasel eyeballed Cady. "Why'd you make that bet? You know something we don't?"

She cut a quick glance at Kix. "I liked the name. It reminded me of somebody."

"Jesus," Red repeated.

Jimmy snorted, then took a bite out of a king-sized candy bar.

Ernie shook his head and mumbled, "Beginner's luck."

"Let me ask you guys something," Cady said after the three men had decided how they were going to place their bets in the third race.

"Go ahead, my good lady," Ernie said.

"Have you heard anything about horses turning up with cocaine in their systems?"

Jimmy got a sour look on his face. "Happened Thursday. I had tickets on two of the horses that came in fourth." He spat on the ground. "Maybe I'd have been in the money if those winning horses hadn't been running on dope. But the way the track works, betting is done in real-time, so they pay out when the horse wins. The trainer gets in trouble if they find out afterward that the horse was dirty."

Red gave him a sympathetic look. "Damn fool woman trainer."

Cady felt Kix tense and automatically put her hand on his arm. For a minute she was distracted by the heat pouring off of him and shooting straight to her cunt. Damn, touching him was like touching molten gold. She shook her head clear of the image. "Why do you think it was the trainer who did it? That seems like it would be pretty stupid." Cady winked at Red. "Even for a woman."

The old man actually turned as red as the feather in his cowboy hat. Before he could answer, Jimmy jumped into the conversation, "Something fishy about it, that's for sure. Never seen anything like it. Five horses in a day!"

Ernie nodded. "The word on the backstretch is that somebody doesn't like Adrienne McKay."

Excitement zipped through Cady. "Any idea who?"

Ernie shook his head. "Haven't heard any names."

Cady leaned forward. "But you think somebody doped her horses so she'd get suspended?"

Ernie shrugged. "Can't figure out anything else that makes sense. There's a rule says that a trainer is a hundred percent responsible for their horses. It's to keep racing clean. Trouble is, it's a nightmare for the trainer. Say the trainer sacks some groom for not doing his job. Well, if the groom gets pissed, he could slip something to a horse and ruin the trainer."

Of course, Cady knew about the Trainer Insurer Rule, but she didn't let on. "Won't the racing officials investigate and try to find out what really happened?"

Jimmy shook his head. "Not their job."

"Sounds pretty unfair." Cady looked at Ernie. "Any guesses who would want to see McKay suspended?"

Jimmy snorted. "Probably happened because somebody don't like that jockey by the same last name."

"Yeah, she's got a real chip on her shoulder." Red hadn't gotten his two cents in for a while. "She's pissed off that she wasn't born a man. Got the personality of a rabid dog."

Cady only barely contained her laugh at hearing Kix's analogy coming out of Red.

Red said, "Fighting ain't becoming of a woman."

Jimmy snorted. "But she sure whipped that other jockey's ass good. What was his name?"

"Valdez," Ernie answered.

"One thing for certain," Jimmy continued, "I'm not going to put any money on that Valdez. Getting whipped by a girl jockey. Bad enough when the girl beats 'em on horseback but when she takes him down using her fists — what's the world coming to?"

The announcer's voice interrupted the conversation. The time for getting bets in for the third race was almost over. Since Cady wanted to cash in her ticket, she said, "I'll take the bets this time."

Jimmy just handed her a five-dollar bill, "Put it on whatever horse you're betting on. But go to show."

Red rolled his eyes. "Jesus, Jimmy, have some bal — guts. Have some guts for a change."

Jimmy didn't seem the least bit offended. "Got to stick to my strategy."

Ernie the Weasel shook his head and handed Cady a ten. "Tom Cat to win."

Kix chuckled and said, "Mind taking my bet, little darlin'?"

Cady's eyebrows rose. "Let me guess, Tom Cat?"

"Yeah, I like the sound of him." Kix handed her his winning ticket. "Cash it in and bet fifty. I'm starting to feel real lucky."

His smile rolled through her body like an avalanche of ice-hot desire. "In your dreams."

Kix laughed. "Oh yeah, darlin', want to know what's in them?"

She shook her head, beginning to think that maybe the best way to handle him was to just ignore him.

Cady placed the bets then lingered in the grandstand for a few minutes, watching television monitors that were simulcasting races from other tracks. Electronic tellers were strategically positioned so that gamblers could use their ATM or credit cards to place bets on anything running—even the races from Hong Kong.

She shook her head and started back to where the men were, thinking how good it was that early on, when Bulldog had started teaching his grandchildren how to play poker and to gamble, he'd always insisted they use real money. There'd been some painful lessons when a week's worth of allowance ended up in someone else's pocket. But in the end they'd all internalized Bulldog's Golden Rule—figure out how much you're willing to spend on your gambling entertainment before you pick up the first card—and don't pay a penny more.

"Thought you might have taken our money and run," Red teased when Cady got back. She laughed and handed everyone their tickets.

"Fast Dancing," Jimmy squeaked when he looked at the paper in his hand. "That horse hates to run on a dirt track. He's a grass horse." He thumped on his *Daily Racing Form* as though it was the *Bible*.

Since Cady didn't have any clue what was in the *Racing Form,* she shrugged and argued the first thing that came to mind. "Hey, the trainer must have a reason for making the switch."

Red pushed his hat back. "She's got a point there."

Jimmy grumbled some more. But as soon as the horses paraded out on their way to the starting box he leaned forward to give Fast Dancing another look. The bay gelding wasn't as fiery as Slick Moves had been, but he'd drawn an inside spot at the starting gate. "You might be onto something."

It took a while to get the horses loaded. A gray colt refused to enter the narrow shoot of the starting gate and a battle ensued—five men against one horse. The men won, but only because the horse wasn't totally committed to resisting their efforts.

A second later the horses were out and fighting for a good position on the track. Fast Dancing took an early lead and maintained it. In the end he won by a length.

"Jesus," Red said. "Don't tell me you picked him because of the name."

Cady laughed and cut a quick look at Kix. He was tearing up his ticket, a look of utter disgust on his face.

Ernie the Weasel shook his head. "Beginner's luck."

Jimmy grunted and used the armrests of his chair for leverage as he pulled his bulk out of the seat. "Gotta go cash my ticket in." His face was beet-red from standing up.

Cady joined him on the stairs leading to the interior part of the grandstand. "Do you come here every day?"

"Yep, me and Red and Ernie come every day the track is open, rain or shine."

"What do you think about the protesters out front? Do you think they hurt the track?"

Jimmy laughed. "Young punks. They don't even bother to come except on the weekends. And they don't follow the horses when the meet shifts to Golden Gate Fields."

"How long have they been protesting?"

"Since the beginning of the year." He was huffing and puffing, out of breath by the time they got to the betting window. The cashier counted out his winnings. When Jimmy had it in his hand he brought the bills to his mouth and gave the bundle a big kiss.

Cady laughed and copied his action when she got her wad of cash. "You going to bet the next race?"

Jimmy shook his head. "Never bet the fourth race. It's unlucky for me."

Red came strolling up and heard the comment. He looked at Cady and grinned. "Fourth wife cleaned Jimmy out when she left him. He's never been the same since. Hates the number four." He thrust his program into Cady's hands. "Who you betting on in the fourth? I'm going to put a couple of dollars on your horse."

Cady scanned the names, but none of them caught her eye. "Nothing's coming to me."

"Quit while you're ahead," Jimmy said.

Cady gave Red an apologetic smile. He shrugged, then headed for the window to place his bet.

Jimmy got in line at the snack bar and Cady suppressed a smile, remembering how he'd claimed that he'd start a diet as soon as he started winning. "Have any other trainers been suspended or put on probation for drugged horses lately?" she asked.

"Yeah, a couple of weeks ago Tiny Johnson got a suspension." Jimmy snorted, "Sure took 'em a long time to fix something on him. That guy is as crooked as the day is long."

"Anyone else?"

Jimmy took a minute to order two hot dogs, some fries, and a giant Coke. "Why are you interested?"

"Just curious."

The lady behind the snack bar counter handed Jimmy his order. "Ernie'd probably know what rumors are going around. He buddies up with guys from the backstretch."

Cady ordered a large Diet Coke and a jumbo order of fries, rationalizing that she'd share them with Kix. She was almost sorry she'd done it when she got back to her seat and his smile let her know how much he enjoyed the idea that she'd been thinking of him.

"What did Tiny Johnson get suspended for?" Cady asked Ernie.

"Antihistamines. Got fined and put on suspension for three months."

"Antihistamines? That doesn't sound too bad."

Ernie shrugged. "You never know what kind of penalty is going to come down. He had a horse that had some trouble breathing. So he gave it an antihistamine to clear it up. Course he claimed that he'd done it days before the race. No way of knowing for sure. You want my opinion, the officials were just looking for something to pin on him."

"Jimmy says the guy is as crooked as the day is long. Is that why they wanted to get him on something?"

"Naw, just politics. The Johnson family owns a lot of stock in the track. They're a big family, but seems they're always at each other's throats."

The horses came out of the saddling enclosure and loosened up before parading to the starting gate. Cady couldn't think of anything else to ask, so she pulled out her camera and started taking pictures.

"Want to walk around a bit?" Kix suggested after she'd shot a roll of film and loaded a fresh one.

"Sure."

They stood, saying their goodbyes and shaking hands with Miguel's friends. When Ernie offered his, Cady felt the cool, smooth texture of paper.

"The track's an interesting place," Ernie said. "Always a lot of things happening, my good lady. A person just has to know who to ask when they're gathering information."

Cady pulled her hand away, keeping the piece of paper locked inside until she and Kix were out of sight. When she finally looked, she found that she was holding the corner of Ernie's race program. There was a name written on it. Roberto Gonzalez.

"Not bad, little darlin', not bad at all." Kix pulled her into his arms and nuzzled along her neck, sending tiny pulses of pure desire through Cady's body. "I think maybe I'm going to have to deputize you." His hand moved around to cup her ass and mold her against his erection. "Then I'll have to show you the proper handling and use of all the equipment."

Cady's pussy spasmed, and for a minute she didn't resist the images unfolding in her imagination. She felt like she was getting ready to ride right over a cliff but she couldn't stop the horse she was on. "Where to next?"

"Right now my stomach is begging for something more than french fries. You up for pizza?"

The fries were already a memory as far as Cady's stomach was concerned. She pulled away from Kix. "Pizza sounds good. I don't know this area very well, but there's a pizza place near my house."

"Why don't we pick one up and take it to your place? Adrienne's attending some big event with Alex tonight, and I sure would hate to end up trapped in her house with Terry."

"Somehow that doesn't worry me too much. I thought you held your own against her."

He grinned. "You're not afraid of being alone with me, are you? Scout's honor, darlin', I'll behave myself over pizza and we'll talk about the case."

Cady had the sinking feeling that she might have stepped right into a trap, but that didn't stop her heart from doing a happy dance in her chest at prolonging their time together. "Were you even a Boy Scout?"

Kix flashed an irresistible smile. "First you question my manhood, now you're questioning my honor. Where I come from, that'd be cause for a shootout at noon."

Cady rolled her eyes, but she couldn't keep a smile from escaping. Oh boy, she was in trouble. "All right—but only because of the case…that's the sole reason I'm taking you home with me."

Kix's cock jumped in celebration—and anticipation. His little darlin' might be telling herself that the only reason she was inviting him home was the case, but her body knew different. It was practically begging to be roped and gentled — by him.

Chapter Four

As soon as they pulled up in front of Cady's house, she knew she was going to have to throw together a salad, otherwise there'd never be enough pizza to go around. She grimaced. Sometimes there was a downside to the company housing that Bulldog provided. It was great when it came to security and companionship—but when it came to bringing members of the opposite sex home, well…

Erin and Lyric both came sailing out of the house next door, Erin's house, before Cady could even get her front door open. Lyric took one look at Kix and said, "You must be the cowboy. No wonder Alex is worried. I'm Lyric."

Kix's laugh rolled right through Cady and squeezed her heart. She took a deep breath, determined not to get upset if he decided to make a play for one of her sisters.

"It's Kix, right?" Erin asked, not that she ever forgot a name. "I'm Erin."

"Kix Branaman, at your service, ladies."

Cady's eyes flew to his face. Just because she hadn't heard a sexual innuendo in the word *service* didn't mean there wasn't one. Their eyes met. His opened a little wider and then he grinned, as though he'd figured out exactly what she'd been thinking.

"Have you guys eaten?" Cady asked.

Lyric looked at the pizza box Kix was carrying. "Not yet."

"I'll help with the salad," Erin said.

As they ate dinner, Cady and Kix filled her sisters in about their day at the track. Kix's behavior surprised Cady. She'd expected him to flirt outrageously with Lyric and Erin—or at least do his cowboy routine, complete with sexy drawl and lanky sprawl. But as they talked about the case, she could easily imagine Kix as a sheriff. He was serious, professional and thoughtful—none of which did anything to put a hold on her erotic fantasies.

"Not a lot of leads—except for this guy, Roberto Gonzalez," Erin said as she helped clear the table. "Why'd Ernie slip you a note and not just tell you flat-out?"

Cady shrugged. "I don't know. Jimmy said that Ernie likes to hang around with some of the guys on the backside of the track. Maybe Ernie guessed what we were investigating and didn't want to say anything openly since we hadn't."

Lyric frowned. "Could be. So you'll be hunting down Gonzalez tomorrow?"

Cady nodded. "I'm trying to decide whether or not to go over to the racing office and ask some questions."

Lyric stood and moved over to the counter, opening a drawer and pulling out a deck of cards and some poker chips. "Why not stay below the radar screen? Hang out as a professional photographer and snoop around."

Erin nodded. "The protestors jumped on that one— and besides, you are a professional photographer. You've done some work on the track before, right?"

"A couple of times. But there's still the connection to Bulldog."

Lyric shrugged. "So? People might wonder whether or not you're also investigating, but if you don't say you are, then they won't know for sure. Let Kix hit the office."

Cady looked at Kix. "What do you think?"

He flashed the sexy Texas smile. "Teamwork, darlin' — you go with the photographer cover story while I mosey over to the office and introduce myself...maybe even pull out the badge and polish it."

Cady could see him doing it. Then again, if the office was staffed with women — they might be more interested in seeing him polish something else. Her eyes did an involuntary drop but the table cut off her view.

Kix chuckled and blood rushed to Cady's face. She turned her head, not wanting to see the knowing look in his eyes.

Lyric brought the cards and chips back to the table. "Do you play, Kix?"

"As a matter of fact, I play a mean game of poker. I was telling Cady about it earlier today. Deal me in."

They played until Lyric had to leave, followed a few minutes later by Erin.

"Anything I can do to help?" Erin asked at the front door.

Cady remembered the rolls of film she'd shot at the track. "Are you going to be doing any darkroom work?"

"On my way over there as soon as I hit the Starbucks. You want me to process the stuff you shot today?"

"That'd be great." Cady retrieved the rolls and handed them to Erin as Kix joined them at the door.

"I'll leave the proof sheets on your desk." Erin grimaced. "You won't see me again until late tomorrow evening. I've got a full day, plus I've got to go to San Francisco tomorrow."

"The interview for the dog show?" Cady asked.

Erin sighed. "Yeah, wish me luck."

Cady gave her sister a hug. "Good luck, but they're crazy if they don't hire you on the spot."

As soon as the door closed behind Erin, Kix pulled Cady against his body. "Alone at last, darlin'."

She shivered at the feel of his erection against her pelvis, at the heat pouring off his skin, and the hungry look in his eyes. "I could take you back to Adrienne's," she said, though her body protested the thought of him leaving.

Kix chuckled before nuzzling along the side of her neck. "I reckon it'd take a posse of deputies to drag me away now that I've got you where I want you."

Cady's own laugh was shaky. "What about the Boy Scout promise?"

Kix pressed an open-mouthed kiss to her neck, ending with a sucking little bite that sent a sharp spike of need streaking to Cady's already swollen clit. "I think if you check the record, darlin', I promised to behave myself over pizza and while we were talking about the case." He sucked her earlobe into his mouth before moving to trace the delicate shell of her ear. "Pizza's gone and we're done talking about the case."

He lifted his head and Cady almost whimpered at the intensity of his gaze. No one had ever looked at her like that. No one had ever been so open about wanting her or used such an irresistible mix of humor and raw sexuality.

Kix gave her plenty of time to escape, but Cady was beyond pretending. She was achy, needy—had been all day. Her clit was as swollen and sensitive as her nipples were, but more that that, she wanted — at least this once — to just "go for the gusto" as Lyric liked to say.

Cady met him halfway, moaning softly as their lips touched. Kix moved into her, holding her against the door as he sucked on her bottom lip. She arched into him, pressing her breasts into his chest. Kix groaned and slid his hands between them, unbuttoning her shirt.

Wet heat pooled between Cady's thighs and she couldn't stop herself from spreading her legs wider so that she could cradle and rub his cock. Kix panted, then stroked his tongue into her mouth in the same rhythm as his cock moved against her clothing-protected mound.

The need for air finally drove them apart. "Darlin', you're like a shot of whisky," Kix said, his eyes moving to where her shirt hung open.

Cady watched his face as he undid the front clasp of her bra and freed her breasts. "Beautiful," he whispered, his eyes darkening as his thumbs rubbed over her nipples.

Her womb fluttered, sending a rush of liquid to her panties. She whimpered, begging for more when his callused hands cupped her breasts, lifting them and pressing them together.

He took the nipples between his fingers, alternating between soft flicks and nearly painful squeezes. Her lower body pressed more tightly against his.

Kix laughed softly, tightening his fingers on her nipples. "You like that, don't you, darlin'?" He released his hold on one nipple, then bent over and lapped the areola before sucking it into his mouth.

Cady's hands flew to his head. Her fingers buried themselves in his hair and held him to her breast as she arched, offering him more, wanting him to bite and suck and swallow her whole.

He switched to the other breast, one hand holding it firmly as he suckled while the other hand made quick work of opening her jeans and burrowing into her panties. His cock jerked at the wet feel of her against his fingers.

It was all he could do not to drag Cady down to her hands and knees and rut on her like a half-crazed bull. The only thing keeping him from doing it was the fact that he wanted to bury his head between her legs and taste the honey that was coating his fingers.

Cady whimpered and flooded his hand with more of her desire—her need. He groaned and pulled back, his face tight, his eyes heated. "Cady darlin', I'm not sure how long I'm going to last once I start riding you. I've been needing you since the minute you walked into Adrienne's office." He dragged his finger along her wet slit and over her clit before pulling his hand from her jeans.

Instinctively Cady's body tried to follow his finger. She arched into him. "Oh god, don't stop."

Kix leaned in so that his lips hovered over hers. "Tell me what you want, darlin'. Do you want me to lap up your cream and suck your clit until you scream? Or do you want me to shove my tongue into your sweet little channel and fuck you with it 'til you come?"

Cady grip tightened in his hair. "All of it, I want you to do it all."

His hands moved to her waistband and he pushed her jeans and panties down. Then he paused for a moment, just savoring the first sight of her—the neatly shaped brown triangle of pubic hair, the plump swollen lips of her sex, the clit standing erect—begging for his mouth.

With a groan he knelt down in front of her, cupping the soft skin of her buttocks and pulling her tight as he buried his face in her pussy. Heaven. The smell of her, the taste of her. He attacked her like a starving man—licking and sucking and biting and thrusting with his tongue—relishing the sound of her whimpers, the cries and pleas, and finally the sound of her screaming his name as she came.

Kix pulled away, his face flushed, his breath moving in and out of his chest like a racehorse in the home stretch. "I don't think I can make it past the living room, darlin'."

They stopped short of the couch, stripping out of their clothes and going down to the floor in a tangle of arms and legs as they struggled to get as much skin-to-skin contact as possible. Kix's body was everything Cady had fantasized it would be—his cock swollen and thick, its head flushed and wet.

His mouth went back to her breasts, kissing and sucking and licking as though they were a temptation he couldn't resist. Cady reached for his penis, stroking along the shaft before moving to the sensitive head. He groaned, wetting her palm with drops of pre-cum. She used the moisture to tease him until his hand cupped hers and his hips humped up and down, sliding his cock in and out of their combined grip.

His strokes grew faster, more forceful, until he groaned and jerked out of her grip, his own hand still on his cock, trying to stave off orgasm rather than achieve it. Cady was entranced by the sight, by the pleasured agony she saw in his face. "Kix," she whispered.

He huffed out a breath, feeling like a stud put to his first mare. "Cady darlin', I can't hold off much longer. He reached for his jeans and pulled out a foil packet, ripping it open with his teeth.

"Let me do it."

Kix groaned at the look on her face. "Not this time, darlin'. I won't last if you touch me again." She leaned in, mesmerized by the sight of him smoothing the condom over his erection.

When he was done, he gathered her in his arms and lay back, pulling her on top of him, then rolling so that she was underneath him, legs spread, her cunt cradling his throbbing penis. When she wrapped her legs around his hips, it was all he could do to keep from driving home in one stroke and pounding into her.

But he wanted to take it slow, wanted to savor this first time with her. So he leaned in, covering her mouth with his, tempting her tongue to come out and play—to dance and twine and thrust until she was whimpering and grinding and finally tilting so that in one smooth, perfectly choreographed move, his cock slipped inside her.

They stilled for a heartbeat—eyes locked, trapped in an instant of perfect unity—and then neither could hold back any longer.

A fever gripped Kix and all he could think about was driving into Cady, pounding into her and filling himself with the sounds of her pleasure. Something primitive inside of him screamed for him to stop and rip the latex barrier away so the he could feel his woman's tight little channel as it gripped him. He fought the urge by going deeper. His thrusts becoming more frantic, as did hers. When she orgasmed, he joined her, shaking and snorting and groaning like a stallion breeding a mare as a wash of lava-hot semen rushed through his cock.

They lay entwined for several moments afterward, Cady's fingers mimicking his as they stroked along his backbone and the base of his spine. "I hope you don't expect me to jump up and drive you back to Adrienne's house right away," Cady teased and his heart blossomed with warmth at the underlying uncertainty he heard in her voice. Damn, she was so refreshingly honest.

Kix brushed a kiss along her neck. "That's just the warm up, darlin'. I haven't fully deputized you."

She laughed and shifted so they faced each other. "You think maybe I'm not familiar enough with the equipment yet?"

"Not by a long shot." He gave her a quick kiss. "Ready for bed, darlin'?"

"I want a shower first."

Kix grinned. "I like the sound of that."

Cady heated up another couple of degrees. "It's not a very big shower."

"We'll double up."

They moved to the bathroom and Cady flushed. It was a favorite fantasy of hers, but now she felt awkward. Kix pulled her against his body. "You want me to braid up this pretty mane of hair so it won't get wet?" She shivered and nodded. He rubbed the side of his face against her hair, then made quick work of getting the wild curls under control.

Cady stepped into the shower and grabbed the bar of soap. Kix followed her, holding his hand out, but she shook her head. "My turn first."

God, what a gorgeous body. For a long minute all Cady could do was stare at it. There wasn't an ounce of fat anywhere, and everything was perfectly proportioned.

Her attention moved to his cock and when it gave a little leap of recognition, Cady's gaze flew to Kix's face. Heat flooded her cunt at the lazy smile and appreciative look in his eyes.

She lathered up her hands, dropping the bar of soap before slowly stroking over his smooth chest. His penis jumped again. His nipples went to tight little points, and when Cady smoothed her fingers over them, he groaned and stepped into her, pressing his now-erect cock against her water-slick skin.

She flicked her thumbs over the nipples, then moved so the water would wash away the soap before she leaned forward and laved the sensitive points with her tongue. Kix groaned and wrapped his arms around her, holding her against him.

Cady tortured him as he'd tortured her, moving from one nipple to the next as she used her fingers and tongue, and the suction of her mouth to drive him higher.

When he was panting and grinding his pelvis against her, she moved her assault lower—first trailing her hands down his sides and abdomen—then following with her mouth.

His cock pulsed and jerked against her cheek, demanding attention as Cady knelt, exploring the smooth flesh over the rock-hard firmness of Kix's abdomen. She leaned away from him and looked up—going hot and needy at the feral, hungry expression on Kix's face as he looked down at her.

Kix braced his hands against the walls of the shower, trying to keep them from grabbing her and holding her so that he could get his cock into her hot little mouth. Every cell in his body was tense with anticipation—and fear that she wouldn't give him what he was suddenly sure he needed to have in order to survive. "Cady, darlin'…" It was a guttural plea that he couldn't stop from escaping.

Cady's face flushed and she whispered, "I've never done it before. You'll have to tell me what you like."

Fire raced through Kix's cock. Primitive satisfaction rushed through his heart and soul.

His penis twitched and Cady leaned forward, tentatively circling the flared, pulsing head with her tongue. Kix bucked involuntarily and closed his eyes against the pleasure she was giving him. Damn, but he just wanted to lose himself in her.

Her mouth widened, inviting him in with small sucks, and he began pumping in short strokes. Her hands went to his hips and his buttocks clenched. The low moans she was making as she sucked, pulling him deeper with each thrust, had his balls pulling tight against his body. Against his will, the pressure began to build, warning him that he wouldn't last much longer.

As much as he wanted to come that way, he wanted to be inside her tight, hot pussy more. With a groan he pulled away, panting, "I'm too close, Cady darlin'."

"It would have been okay," Cady said, flushing adorably and sending a shaft of pure happiness through Kix.

He pulled her to her feet, hugging her to him. "Another time, darlin', you can bet the entire pot on it. Right now I got something better in mind."

Cady smiled against his shoulder. "I didn't think anything was better than a blowjob to a guy."

Kix laughed. "Well, it's right up there—I'd be lying if I said it wasn't. But ever since you told me you liked to ride,

I've been fantasizing about having your hot little body riding mine."

Cady pressed a kiss against his wet skin. "I've had that same fantasy."

"Well, darlin' let's go for a ride."

Afterward, Kix wrapped himself around a sleeping Cady and wondered how it had happened. There'd been no warning, no way of seeing it coming. Somehow, he'd been sucker punched. But the unfamiliar feelings chasing around in his heart like a dog after its tail didn't leave any room for being mad.

He ought to be fighting like a bull that had been roped and thrown down for branding. Instead he was awake, curled up around a woman—his woman—worrying about whether or not he was going to be able to keep her safe if this investigation went sideways.

Damn, he didn't like the feel of what was going on at the track, couldn't get his head around the crime, or what the person setting Adrienne up was after. It didn't make any sense, so there was no way of knowing how it would play out—whether things would get uglier and turn more dangerous.

Kix rubbed his chin on the top of Cady's head and she mumbled something in her sleep, snuggling even closer and sending a fresh wave of heat through him when her ass wriggled against his penis. "Damn, you're a distraction, Cady darlin'. But I don't think I can do without you."

Chapter Five

As far as Erin was concerned, San Francisco was a claustrophobic's nightmare. Wall-to-wall buildings blocked out most of the sky and there were too many cars, too few parking places, a meter maid on every block, and way too many people. She felt like she was going to hyperventilate as soon as she drove into the city, but the prospect of landing the job as the official photographer for the big Cow Palace show had her trolling for a parking place, feeding the meter, and then pushing through crowds of people in order to get to Bob Levy's office.

She'd never met Levy, but she knew he was an important man in the dog show world—a past president of the American Kennel Club and an avid long-time fancier of pugs. The Cow Palace Show was *the* dog show event of the West Coast, and the San Francisco kennel club putting it on was a prestigious one. Membership came via birthright, not by filling out an application and sending in a fee. She was only here because one of her clients had put in a good word for her when the kennel club's usual show photographer was ousted as a result of club politics.

Erin crossed her fingers as she made her way into Levy's reception area. It'd be a real coup if she could get the job. And there was plenty of work to pull Cady in, too.

She bit her lip at the thought of her sister. The heat sizzling between Cady and the cowboy had been enough to turn the air in Cady's house downright sultry. Erin hoped that Cady knew what she was doing.

Until now, Cady had always been more like her—cautious when it came to the opposite sex. Lyric, on the other hand, had always boldly gone where no sensible woman would go.

Erin shivered. Oh yeah, caution was a good thing. She only had to look as far as Lyric's new husband to confirm that. Kieran oozed alpha male—the kind that practically sweat testosterone and dominance—not that Lyric didn't give him a run for his money and enjoy every second of it. In other words, they were perfect for each other.

But no thanks. No thanks to a dominating male. And in particular, no thanks to any male in the law enforcement profession. No cops—especially vice cops like Kieran—no private investigators—she'd seen her male cousins in action—and no bounty hunters. She didn't want to have to worry every time her husband left for work that something would happen to him and he wouldn't make it home.

A door opened and Erin forced her thoughts to the upcoming interview as Levy ushered her into his office. He was younger than she'd expected. But the old adage about people looking like their dogs, or vice versa, proved true. Pudgy, bald headed, and short-nosed, Levy looked a lot like the breed he'd spent a lifetime promoting—pugs.

Erin placed her portfolio on Levy's desk before taking her seat. Levy settled into a heavily padded chair and immediately took the offered collection of photographs and began flipping through them. He finished and placed the portfolio back on his desk just as Erin's chair had finally molded to her shape. Her heart dropped to her feet. It had been years since someone had rejected her so quickly.

Levy looked up. "Beautiful work. The job's yours if you want it."

Shock held Erin silent for a long minute. "That's it? Just like that?"

He nodded and smiled. "I've seen your work hanging on a few walls. The portfolio just confirmed what I already thought. I assume you want the job."

"I'd love to do the show."

"Good, good." He looked at his watch. "I've got to get to another meeting." He picked up a manila envelope and handed it to Erin. "My secretary prepared a package of information for you. Look it over. Give me a call if you have any questions." He rose from his chair. Erin followed suit. Both of them were startled when they heard a roar of angry voices from outside his window.

Levy frowned and stalked over to look outside. "Damn protesters."

Erin joined him at the window. The view from his office was much different than the one she'd seen when she entered on the other side of the building. Below them there must have been two hundred screaming, sign-toting protesters—ringed by an equally impressive number of blue-uniformed policemen.

She grimaced. She did not miss the three-hundred-and-sixty-seven days and five hours that she'd been a cop. "What are they protesting?"

"Today it's anti-fur." Levy snorted. "What a mess. No point in even being at the office. Clients don't want to come in. Noise gets so bad you can't even hear yourself think."

Another wave of chanting rippled through the crowd. Erin scanned the scene one more time, wondering if there were any shots worth wading in for. She did a double take when she saw the man at the front of the crowd. He looked just like the guy Cady had photographed at Bay Downs. She closed her eyes, concentrating on seeing the pictures she'd developed for Cady last night. She was pretty good with faces and the one in the protest below matched the one in her mind's eye.

As soon as she left Levy's office, she headed for the demonstration. The crowd felt anxious and tense. The policemen who ringed the demonstrators looked dead serious about maintaining order.

In addition to the men who surrounded the protesters, there were several more on horseback, and other men stationed in second-story offices. Erin could see them standing next to open windows, radios in hand, waiting to identify troublemakers.

TV and radio crews mingled with the demonstrators, their microphones and cameras at the ready. Erin suspected that they wouldn't be disappointed. She stopped long enough to get her camera out of its case, then skirted the perimeter of the crowd, trying to get to a point where she could see the protesters at the front.

It was slow going, but when she finally made it, Erin felt a thrill of victory. The man standing at the front of this protest was the same one who'd been leading the Bay Downs group. He may have been going through the motions at Bay Downs, but here he was chanting loudly and hoisting his sign with passion.

Erin dredged up the demonstrator's name—Danny something... Danny Meyers—that was the name on the release form he'd signed. She lifted her camera and started taking pictures. This version of Danny could hold his own against any of the save-a-tree protestors that Kix had joked about.

She'd gone through her first roll of film and was just loading a second when a jockey-sized man pushed through the crowds and came to a stop next to Meyers. From the expression on the protestor's face, he knew the man, but he wasn't happy to see him. They exchanged a few words. Meyers shook his head "no". The jockey-sized man grew angry, his face flushed and he snarled something at the protester. Meyers looked up and around, then handed his sign to the woman next to him. The two men slipped out of the crowd. Erin checked to make sure her film had fed in correctly before following them, her heart thumping with anticipation and nervousness.

She kept her distance, though neither man seemed concerned about being seen together. They were arguing, though Meyers seemed to be doing most of the talking. Five blocks over they came to a halt next to an old orange Volkswagen.

Meyers opened the trunk and retrieved an index-card-sized box. Erin snapped a shot just as he handed the box to the smaller man. They exchanged a few more words then parted company without exchanging anything other than the box.

Erin ducked into an alleyway and waited for them to get out of sight before she returned to the demonstration. Meyers was back to protesting, sign waving high, voice raised in a chant. She watched for a few minutes longer. Then just as she was turning to leave, a woman wearing a long fur coat emerged from the store in front of the protestors.

Erin shook her head, amazed but not amazed, wondering who in their right mind would put on a fur coat and parade in front of demonstrators.

Meyers dropped his sign and pulled a spray can out of his shirt. A second later he lunged toward the woman and before any of the policemen could stop him, he managed to spray blood-red paint across the woman's fur coat.

Another protester dashed in and added his can. The woman stood shrieking and screaming as the crowd roared its approval.

Erin recorded it on film even as she was put off by the sorry melodrama taking place in front of her. Not that she wasn't sympathetic to the cause—she was. But it was a predictable plot, played out time and time again by fur wearers and anti-fur protesters. She wondered how many times the image of a fur coat with blood-red paint had been splashed across the front page of local newspapers. She didn't think it changed anything.

A third man tried to join the other two, but before he could add his paint to the coat, policemen swarmed in and dragged all three men away. Erin figured she'd seen enough. She put her camera back in its case, anxious to call Cady and tell her what she'd seen. She wished there was some way to hand off the film for developing, but it was going to have to wait until evening. She had appointments already scheduled and they were taking her further from home, not closer.

* * * * *

Cady shivered as she thought about waking up snuggled into Kix, his morning erection pressed against her so that all she had to do was shift slightly and he slipped into her already wet slit and began pumping in and out slowly, as though he wanted to put off the moment when they had to get up and start the day.

She'd half expected it would be awkward waking up with him in her bed and having to drive him back to Adrienne's place. It wasn't—and that worried her. Fixing his breakfast and handing him a cup of coffee first thing in the morning felt right—perfect. Giving him a kiss before he got out of her truck and sauntered up Adrienne's walkway only made her anticipate when she'd see him next.

She wasn't sorry she'd gotten involved with him. He made her feel alive, desirable, happy in a way she'd never felt before—and she fully intended to savor every moment, but… A fist tried to tighten around her heart, a warning about how it was going to feel when he was gone.

Cady resolutely pushed the thoughts away.

No regrets. That was going to be her motto. And in the meantime, she had Adrienne's case to work on and portraits to shoot.

Cady met Grady Windburn at the gate to the backside of Bay Downs. He'd hired her to do several portraits of his mother's three Yorkies. The first had been a surprise Christmas gift featuring the three dogs dressed up in sailor suits. His mother had gone crazy over the photos, so Grady had treated her to a second portrait—this one for her birthday—and now a third was scheduled.

When Cady had seen his name in her appointment book, she'd remembered that he owned an interest in a racehorse. The timing couldn't have been more perfect—

especially when he agreed to get her a pass into the backstretch so she could take some photos.

"Who's your trainer?" Cady asked as she and Grady headed toward the collection of shed-rows, each considered a "barn".

"Young guy, Mike Beck, only had his license for a couple of years. But he's hot!"

"How many horses does he have?"

"Seven, including one of his own. My two are claimers, nothing special, but I think I'll be able to trade up with them. His horse is something else. Broke his maiden the first time out of the gate, and he's won two more since then. Horse is named Dynamite Blast. He's a beautiful bay colt."

Grady angled them to small office that had obviously once been a stall. A young guy wearing a red San Francisco 49ers cap was studying a clipboard while he chewed the life out of his gum.

"Is he going to be ready?" Grady asked.

"Sure, sure. He'll be ready." Mike looked up and Grady made the introductions before flicking his wrist, checking the time on his Rolex. "Well kids, I gotta go."

Mike got out of his chair. "Why don't I give you a quick tour of the place? Just tell me to stop if you see something you want to photograph. We can start over at the practice track." He checked his own watch, then spit a huge wad of gum into the trash, almost immediately pulling out a package and unwrapping a fresh piece.

As soon as they got to the practice track, a female exercise rider on a gray mare rode along the rail in front of them. The mare was snorting and prancing—anxious to take on the track. Cady looked around and thought maybe a couple of the other riders were women, too. There hadn't been a single female jockey listed in the racing program she'd gotten on Sunday. When she mentioned it to Mike he shrugged. "Yeah, owners around here are still pretty squirrelly about putting a woman up on their horses on race day."

Cady watched the young rider skillfully control the excited gray mare as they galloped along the track rail. The mare was bucking and fighting every step of the way. "It seems to me that if women are good enough to exercise the horses then they're good enough to race them." She trained her camera on the rider.

"The horses get pretty excited during a race. A lot of owners don't think a woman has the strength to handle a horse in that kind of situation." He held up his hands in surrender before Cady could give her opinion. "I'm not saying I agree. To tell you the truth, I think a woman often times has better hands and a better feel for the horse. But an owner tells me 'no' to a woman jock and I say 'fine'. The owner is paying the bill." He shrugged. "But I do put a lot of women on as exercise riders."

"So there aren't any female jockeys riding at Bay Downs?"

"Just one. Terry McKay."

"Is she any good?"

"Yeah." It came out grudgingly as Mike added a fresh stick of gum to the mix in his mouth. "Hot-headed with the temperament of a junkyard dog. But yeah, she's got a good feel for the horses and for racing."

"Does she have trouble getting rides?"

"Didn't use to. Until last week, she had a lot of rides. Now I doubt she could get on as an exercise rider."

"What happened?"

The gray mare and her rider came by the rail. Mike waved them on. "That's the last one of mine. You want to grab some coffee?"

"Sure."

As they headed back toward the barn housing Mike's office, Cady tried to figure out a way to get back to the subject of Terry McKay. Had he intentionally dropped it, or had he just gotten distracted? Finally she decided to just plow ahead. What the heck, it was a legitimate topic.

"What happened with the female jockey? Did she get caught throwing a race or something?"

Mike laughed. "Naw, nothing like that. Her cousin is a trainer—or I should say, was a trainer. A lot of Terry's mounts came by way of her cousin. Now that Adrienne's been suspended, Terry doesn't have anything to ride, plus people tend to be superstitious. Some of them just don't want to have any trouble rub off on them."

"How come her cousin got suspended?"

A puzzled expression settled on Mike's face. "Five of her horses turned up with cocaine in their system last week."

"Five?"

"Yeah." Mike looked over at Cady. "Pretty damn strange. Most of them had a fair shot at winning—and Adrienne never seemed like the kind of trainer who would drug horses to win. Hell, she doesn't need to as far as that goes. It's pretty common knowledge that she's loaded. Her entire family is loaded. Besides that, she's smart enough to know that the drug test would go positive for cocaine, unless she thought she had it covered from the other end, or was buying something else. Like I said, just doesn't make a hell of a lot of sense."

Cady moved closer. "Sounds like you think someone else might have drugged them."

Mike looked around. "I don't know. I'm just saying that it seems pretty damn strange. Five in a day. You'd have to be damn stupid. A horse wins, it goes right to the stall and they wait to get a urine sample. No exceptions. No surprises. It's not like random drug testing where you figure the odds and decide whether you want to take the chance."

"Did she have any enemies? Anyone who would want to see her kicked off the track? Or do you think somebody was just jealous because she's got money?"

"Who knows?" Mike shrugged. "She's a classy lady. Kind of an outsider since her family's got big bucks and provides her with the horses. Maybe some of the guys are jealous that she's played with the big boys in New Jersey and Florida, but so what? She's a good trainer, keeps kind of to herself. Keeps her nose clean."

"Is she running a particularly good horse right now?"

"They're all good, but nothing like a Cigar or a Secretariat if that's what you mean." They turned between a couple of barns and his office came into sight. "I've got to make a few calls while the coffee is brewing."

"I'll stay out here and take some shots."

The exercise rider returned the gray mare to her groom for a morning bath. Cady edged over and took some pictures before moving to where a bay horse was hooked up to a hot-walker, apparently content to go round and round in the same circle, its lead rope remaining slack as the equipment it was tethered to traveled at a steady pace. Mike joined her a few minutes later and handed her a cup of coffee. "I took a guess that you liked cream and sugar in yours."

"This is great."

They talked about horses as they drank their coffee. When the cups were empty, Mike said, "They should have the tractors and harrows out to recondition the main track about now. You interested in some photos of that?"

"I'm interested in everything."

As they walked in the direction of the main racetrack, she said, "Grady was telling me that Dynamite Blast belongs to you. I saw him run in the fourth race on Sunday."

"He's the best thing that's come my way in a long time. I've already picked up two clients because of him." Mike shook his head. "That's the game. When you're small-time, just starting out, you get two kinds of owners. Cheap ones who can't afford anybody else, and owners that see you've got a winning horse and think you've got some magic that'll work on their old nag."

Cady laughed. "How'd you get into this profession, anyway?"

"Born into it. My old man was a trainer. I did odd jobs on the track when I was growing up. Worked for my dad as a groom. Exercised horses until I got too big. Finally bought a claimer and started trading up."

"Is your dad a trainer here?"

"Naw. He's dead now. Cirrhosis of the liver about five years ago."

"Hard way to lose your father."

"Yeah. My kid won't lose me that way."

"You have kids?"

Mike laughed. "A son, though my wife calls him a demon when he's awake and an angel when he's sleeping."

Cady smiled, betting Mike was a good dad—and instantly picturing Kix in that same role. That thought brought reality crashing back with all the finesse of a thrown rider hitting hard ground.

Her heart contracted. One night of great sex did not make for a future together. She was not going to be sorry, but that didn't mean she was going to get caught up in a happy-ever-after fantasy. As soon as Adrienne's name was cleared, then Kix would head back to Texas. *So don't do anything crazy like falling in love.*

Her chest grew tight and she had the sinking feeling it was too late. How could anyone not fall in love with Kix? He was gorgeous, funny, smart, law-abiding, and loyal to his friends. *Stop!*

Giving herself a mental shake to clear her mind, Cady forced her thoughts out of the circle they'd been going in and began scanning the scene around her, her eyes hitting on a contrast that just begged for a shot—an extraordinarily large, fat in non-politically correct terms, man was talking to a guy who had to be a jockey.

She aimed the camera and zoomed in. Mike followed her interest and laughed. "Yeah, that's quite a sight. The jock is Angel Valdez. He rides a lot of Luke Johnson's horses. The other guy is his agent. Don't know his real name, everybody calls him Fats. It doesn't seem to bother him."

A few shots later, Cady zoomed in closer, trying to capture their expressions. Fats looked angry. His heavy jowls quivered as he talked. He ran a finger along his collar and by the frayed appearance and greasy stains, he did it a lot. The jockey seemed equally angry, his movements more volatile.

"Who'd you say Angel Valdez rode for?" Cady asked when they started walking again.

"Luke Johnson."

"Johnson, that name sounds familiar."

Mike laughed. "It should. Seems like every time you turn around, you run into one of the Johnsons. A lot of Bay Downs stock is owned by them."

"Is it publicly traded?"

"Yep. You can buy it through a broker or from the track office. Most everyone who works for the track owns some shares, but the majority of it is owned by the members of the Johnson family. When it comes right down to it, all the jockeys, agents, grooms, clerks, everybody, could put their stock together and still not override the Johnson vote. That is, if the Johnsons all voted the same way."

"I take it that they don't."

"Not even close. Somebody's always got it in for somebody else."

Cady remembered Jimmy telling her that Tiny Johnson had been suspended. "I take it that Tiny Johnson is one of the Johnsons."

"Yeah. Luke's nephew. They hate each other. But between you and me, they're more alike than different. Tiny is small-time and a lousy trainer. Luke is big-time—has a ton of winners, but also has a ton of horses he blows out—ruins 'um. They end up overseas on somebody's dinner plate. They're not even fit to sell as pleasure horses. In my book, that's a lousy trainer, too."

Cady was just about to agree with Mike's opinion when the piercing sound of a siren blared across the backstretch. She turned around and raw fear shot through her. Dark black smoke was pouring into the air.

Chapter Six

A fire engine raced along the road, passing Cady and Mike as they rounded a shed-row and saw that a barn was on fire. Men were yelling in Spanish and English as some led frantic horses out of their stalls while others used garden hoses to try and contain the flames as the fire engine hooked up to a hydrant and prepared to douse the area.

Cady slipped the lens cap off her camera and chronicled the events taking place in front of her. Within minutes the firemen had won the battle against the fire. It took several minutes longer before onlookers began turning away and returning to their own business.

A man wearing a stopwatch around his neck stopped next to her. "Damn grooms, they know better than to cook in the tack rooms. This could have turned into a fucking nightmare," he said before stomping away.

Cady lowered her camera and turned toward Mike. He halted a heavy-set man and asked, "You know if any of the horses were hurt, Caesar?"

"They all got out okay. Somebody saw it in time. I heard there were only about fifteen horses in there—the rest are either off at other meets or on the practice track. Could have been a hell of a lot worse. It could have jumped over to Luke's barn. He's got all forty stalls filled." The man shook his head. "That's three fires since January. The cooking in the tack rooms has got to stop. We all need to tow the line on this one, Mike. I've told my guys they're history if I catch them doing it."

Mike nodded and the other man walked away. Cady took a small notebook out of her back pocket. "Whose barn is it?"

"Six trainers share it. Tony Silva, Jason Randal, Dennis Hess and Ed Patterson all have about five horses each. Jamie Johnson and Alex Harrison have another ten apiece." Mike turned to Cady. "You want to see anything else?"

She checked her watch and shook her head. It was almost time to meet Kix. "Not today. I've got a photo shoot I need to get to. Thanks for showing me around. I really appreciate it."

"Hey, anytime. Can you find your way out?"

"Yeah, thanks."

Cady's pulse jumped at the sight of Kix leaning in cowboy splendor against the guard booth. When he flashed his lazy smile and pulled her into his arms, her heart started doing a great imitation of a pogo stick routine in her chest.

"Perfect timing, darlin'."

She couldn't resist brushing a kiss across his lips. He countered the move by pulling her tighter and holding her head so that he could delve in and out of her mouth, tangling his tongue with hers and sending blood and heat straight to her cunt.

"Damn, Cady darlin', I missed you."

Her heart leaped, but she wrinkled her nose and said, "I didn't drop you off at Adrienne's house that long ago."

"Darlin', you can't give a man a straight shot of fine whisky and expect him to walk away without wanting another taste." His words licked over her nipples, making them tighten into hard points. She shivered, remembering how his mouth and tongue had felt against her flesh.

Cady's attention dropped to where his jeans-covered erection was pressed against her. Her thoughts followed. Maybe they could take a little break...

Then she remembered why she couldn't. She really did have a photo shoot. Somehow she couldn't picture herself calling her client and saying, *Sorry to cancel on you. Something really big has come up and I've got to get it inside me before I die of unsatisfied lust.*

"What'd you find out about Roberto Gonzalez?" Cady asked.

"He's an assistant trainer working for Tiny Johnson."

Cady's eyebrows went up. "The guy who was suspended because his horse had antihistamines in its system?"

Kix grinned. "One and the same."

"Does Adrienne know him?"

"Yep, says he's a lousy trainer—but can't think why he'd have a grudge against her. Seems to be an equal opportunity hater."

"Have you talked to Tiny?"

"Not yet, little darlin'."

"What about with Roberto Gonzalez?"

Kix shook his head. "Funny thing, they've both gotten mighty scarce since I started asking for them."

Cady nibbled on her bottom lip and Kix closed his eyes against the surge of lust that went through his cock.

Damn but he wanted to suck on her lip, her nipples, the flesh over her abdomen, her clit, her… Hell, the truth of the matter was that he wanted to run his lips and tongue over every inch of skin.

"Do you think they already heard that you were investigating for Adrienne?"

It took Kix a minute to get his mind out of her pants and reconnect with the conversation. He forced his eyes upward, to meet hers, and took satisfaction in the way her cheeks were flushed. "Hard to say. Some crooks have enough savvy to stay ahead of the law—at least in the short term. Tiny and Gonzalez may have something else going and they're worried about me finding out about it."

"Did you flash your badge?"

"Didn't need to." Kix couldn't resist. He leaned forward and brushed his lips against hers. "A little bit of Texas charm and those ladies in the race office were practically throwing answers at me."

Cady didn't know whether to feel depressed or amused. In some part of her brain last night—some very small, non-hormone-overwhelmed part—she'd known that sleeping with him was going to complicate things. Just because he'd had enough sense not to flirt with Erin and Lyric didn't mean that he wasn't going to turn on the charm when someone else caught his eye.

His heart gave a little kick at the expression on her face and he leaned down, taking her bottom lip between his, sucking on it gently before saying, "'Course, they just got interrogation-variety charm." He pressed his erection against her and closed his eyes briefly when her body softened, cradling him. Damn if the fit wasn't just plain perfect. "I save the real firepower for you."

Cady laughed and gave him a hug before stepping back. "Speaking of fires, were you still on the backstretch when the barn was burning?"

"No. Heard the sirens, but I was in the grandstand. They have a cause?"

"Not an official one, though I guess the consensus is that one of the grooms was cooking." Her eyebrows drew together. "I heard someone say it's the third fire since January. That seems like a lot of fires."

Kix shrugged. "Maybe. It would depend on what the grooms were cooking with. Hot plates or camp stoves wouldn't be a good mix with hay and barns. I'll ask Addy about it."

"Did you learn anything interesting when you were charming the ladies in the office?"

"Nothing to share yet."

Cady frowned, not liking the sound of that. Did that mean she was good enough to sleep with, but not good enough to really partner up with on the case? Her heart took a step back. Maybe she should settle for one memorable night and leave it at that. She'd known that having sex with him would only complicate things.

"I've got to head out to do some photo shoots. I guess I'll see you tomorrow."

Something was going on in his little darlin's mind, but damned if Kix knew what to do about it right now. He had a couple of leads he wanted to explore but he didn't want to draw her into it until he knew it was safe. Then after he checked those out, he had to get back to Adrienne's place in order to get spiffed up for a fancy owner-trainer function up in San Francisco. It was just the kind of thing he hated going to, but he figured it would be a prime opportunity to meet, mingle, ask questions—and hopefully come up with a motive behind the drugging of Addy's horses. But that didn't mean he wanted to sleep alone tonight—or with anyone but Cady.

He brushed the fingers of one hand through her wild curls. "I don't know what time I'm going to get back from San Francisco, but if it's not too late, I'd like to come by your place."

She hesitated for a minute, which got his heart to pounding a little harder than he felt comfortable with, but finally she said, "I'd like that, too."

* * * * *

It was close to sunset by the time Cady got done with her scheduled photo shoots. She felt good about all of them, which was in sharp contrast to how she was feeling about the thing with Kix now that she had time to think about it again. Why had she told him that she'd like to see him tonight? What had happened to her resolve to take one great night of sex and call that good?

A quiver in her cunt and a tightening of her nipples was answer enough. Okay, one great night of sex was about a million nights too few when it came to Kix. But that didn't mean... Cady sighed, not willing to lie to herself. She had a bad feeling that when it came to the cowboy sheriff from Texas, she was already a lost cause.

She'd just regroup a little. She'd concentrate on working the angles she came up with and she'd try to remember that her client, the Crime Tells' client, was Alex Martin. If she kept that in mind then she wouldn't feel compelled to tell Kix everything...not unless he was going to share information equally with her. And in the meantime, if they enjoyed each other's company...well, that was fine. As far as she knew, there was no rule that said she couldn't go for the gusto and work a case at the same time. Look at Lyric...

Cady's thoughts came to a screeching halt and she laughed. Maybe that wasn't a good place to look. Lyric had ended up with Kieran when she'd mixed hot sex with one of her cases.

Not that Cady didn't absolutely adore her new brother-in-law, she did. The man was great for Lyric and a total stud muffin to boot. But he was not exactly easygoing. And if he had a sense of humor, then you'd have to dig through a lot of layers of testosterone and alpha-male dominance in order to find it.

No thanks.

Her fantasies did not run along the same lines as Lyric's did... A shiver cut that lie off. Okay, so the thought of being handcuffed to the bed had entered her mind a time or two. And the thought of a spanking—not that she was sure she'd like it—but, yeah, she wouldn't mind seeing what it was all about. And having a guy go in where no man was probably ever meant to go...

So she was curious. Curiosity was a natural thing.

And Lyric's tales had only made it worse.

Maybe next time she played cards with Lyric and Erin, and the losers had to tell their latest sexual exploit, then she'd actually have something to relate!

Then again, was doing more with Kix really a smart thing?

Cady pulled the truck into the gravel parking lot at Hermosa Ranch. What she needed was some horse time to clear her head.

The ranch was made up of two huge, hilly pastures, one for mares and one for geldings. Some days you could spend forty minutes just finding your horse. But today Cady was lucky. Joker was with a small band of ten horses all hanging around the gate.

She grabbed a halter and rope from the back of the truck and went to catch the palomino gelding. He nickered and pushed his way through the other herd members in order to get to Cady. Warmth blossomed through her at the greeting.

"There's my beautiful guy." She gave him a kiss on his forehead and scratched his neck before slipping the halter on him. "No time for a ride today, but I'll give you a little grain and get the tangles out of your mane and tail."

Cady took another minute to scratch Dealer's Call, a bay horse that belonged to her cousin Cole, and then Aces High, Erin's chestnut gelding, before leading Joker out of the pasture and down to the tack shed that she shared with Erin and Cole. She tied him to the hitching post and opened the shed. He nickered again as soon as she poured some feed in a bucket.

"Yeah, like you're starving to death." She hooked the bucket to a ring on the hitching post and got out her grooming supplies.

Miguel Hermosa came by just as she was finishing up on Joker's ground length tail. "Hi there, sweetie. You ready to sell that gelding yet?"

Cady grinned, knowing that he was only half joking. Miguel was a horse collector. He couldn't seem to help himself—not that she couldn't understand why.

Horses were beautiful to look at and relaxing to be around. They were less trouble than a boyfriend, and more loyal than one. Plus they were better than a shrink and a lot less expensive. That's what she always told her cousin Braden when he teased her about riding horses instead of men.

"Nope, not ready to sell him yet." She positioned herself so she could comb out Joker's mane, before adding, "There was a fire on the backside today."

"Anybody hurt?"

"No."

"Whose barn?"

Cady pulled the small notebook out of her back pocket. "Tony Silva, Jason Randal, Dennis Hess, Ed Patterson, Jamie Johnson and Alex Harrison. Do you know any of them?"

Miguel snorted. "Only Jamie Johnson, and he's crooked enough to set fire to the barn himself if there was something in it for him. I used to ride for him. Drunk half the time. Surprised he hasn't killed himself with the booze yet."

"He's one of the Johnsons who practically own the track?"

"Yep. There's Jamie and Luke, brothers though you wouldn't know it by the way they hate each other."

"I heard about Luke. He's supposed to be a popular trainer with the owners."

"Yeah. You run a string of forty horses and you're bound to have some winners. But I'm telling you, sweetie, he's a piss-poor trainer. Blows horses out like they're not worth anything. But owners don't see that. All they see is him standing in the winner's circle night after night. So every time he ships a horse off the track 'cause it's broken down, he has some owner ready to fill the empty stall."

Miguel stopped long enough to roll himself a cigarette. "Jamie's nothing to write home about either. He started out with some talent as a horse trainer — but he was never one to pay his dues. If there's a shortcut, Jamie'll knock you down to get to it first."

"How's Tiny related to Luke and Jamie?"

"Nephew. His mother passed away. Don't know much about him. He was just a youngster when I stopped working at the track. But the track's full of Johnsons, a lot of them are second, third cousins." Miguel shook his head. "Don't know most of them anymore, don't want to know them. Once I quit riding the horses, I promised myself two things — that I'd never go back to the track and I'd never take another drink."

Cady headed home a little while later, her thoughts on the Johnson family. It seemed like their name kept coming up over and over again and so far she hadn't heard anything good about any of them. Was it possible that one or more of them didn't like Adrienne McKay and this was their way of running her off the track? Adrienne was in San Francisco, so she couldn't ask her. But there was always the Web. Cady grinned. How had people managed to live and get anything done without the Internet?

* * * * *

This was just the kind of get-together Kix hated. From the outside, it looked like a bunch of beautiful fish swimming around in an expensive aquarium. From the inside, it felt like a grotto full of sharks.

His mother would love it. But then she'd been raised a Nicholson and they damn near owned as many oil fields as the Branamans did. Kix took a sip of whiskey and silently toasted his ancestors. To the Kicking A Ranch.

Home of fine horses, fine cattle, fine men and some mighty fine oil wells. Now if only he could wrap this thing up with Addy's horses and somehow convince Cady that she had a hankering to see Texas.

His cock jumped at the thought of his little darlin' and he pushed away from the bar. The sooner he got to investigating, the faster he could get back to Cady. That look on her face and that small hesitation before inviting him over after he'd finished up here still had him worried.

Prickly as a hedgehog and as skittish as a filly that hadn't been completely gentled yet — damned if that didn't make a near impossible combination to resist. And the fact that she didn't see the oil wells or the badge when she looked at him, well, no wonder he'd practically handed her the rope to tie him with — not that he was some fancy reining horse or trick pony. But there was no point in showing the bronc right out of the chute. His little darlin' needed to know it was safe to get in the saddle before she got the full ride.

Kix angled toward their host, Andy Barwig, the owner of a horse named Expansion. Adrienne had known more about the horse than the owner, but that was no surprise.

Barwig was surrounded by beautiful women and well-dressed men all hanging on his words. "Let's face it," Barwig was saying as Kix slid next to a sleek woman who sent him a look that would do a piranha justice. "We don't have the tradition that goes along with Louisville Downs and the Kentucky Derby. We don't even have the name recognition of Del Mar or Santa Anita. The only way horseracing is going to thrive here is if we start seeing it for what it is, a gambling sport, not a spectator sport. Big pots, big name horses, showcase barns for big-time trainers, and simulcast betting around the world, that's where the action and the money is. We can't compete against the card rooms and Indian gaming if we don't make some changes. We've got to wake up or die out."

A couple of the men and women nodded in agreement. The piranha next to Kix used the break in conversation to wet her lips and say, "You don't look like Alex Martin, but I thought I saw you come in with Adrienne." There was just a hint of a pout at the mention of Adrienne's name.

Kix could feel the attention shift to him and decided to go ahead and lay his cards on the table. After the trip to the racing office, he figured there wasn't any point in trying to hide who he was and why he was in town. Smiling genially, he introduced himself and said, "I'm sure you know about Adrienne's little difficulty at the track. Well I'm here to get it straightened out for her."

One of the women tittered behind her hand. "Why, aren't you confident!"

Kix flashed his teeth at her, though anyone with half a brain could see that the smile didn't go near his eyes. "Comes with being a sheriff, a Texan and a Branaman, ma'am."

That brought another round of titters and a rub of a breast against his shoulder from the female piranha next to him. A man to the right of Barwig, Luke Johnson, if Kix wasn't mistaken, nodded. "Well, good luck. I don't think anyone in this room really believes that Adrienne had anything to do with drugging her horses. Still…the rules are important. We're in a tough, competitive environment these days. We've got to keep the sport honest."

Kix's eyes were every bit as hard as his voice. "I couldn't agree more. Keeping things honest is important.

That's why I've made a career out of enforcing the law and seeing lawbreakers brought to justice."

* * * * *

Cady's heart jumped when the doorbell sounded. And even though she was happy to see Erin with the roll of film that she'd shot at the anti-fur protest, Cady couldn't hide a flutter of disappointment that it wasn't Kix.

Erin's eyebrows shot up. "Guess you were expecting someone else, huh? I take it he didn't leave last night after Lyric and I did?"

"As if you don't know."

"Well, kind of hard to be sure since you brought him home in your truck." Erin laughed. "Hey, maybe that's where I'm going wrong. Next time I go out with a guy, I'll do the driving, then I can just bring my victim...I mean date, back here...kind of like having a captive audience. They're stuck unless they want to shell out money for a cab or embarrass themselves by calling someone to come pick them up."

Cady shook her head. "If you're trying to make me feel sorry for you so that I'll let you win a hand of poker, forget it. You know you could have any guy you want. I mean, what guy doesn't want someone who looks like a California beach babe. If you would just..."

Erin held up her hand, flashing the film roll in the process. "One more word and I'm not going to give you this."

Cady gave in. When it came to advice on men, anything she could say to Erin, Erin could say right back to her. Between working for Bulldog and trying to build reputations as professional photographers, plus sometimes helping Lyric with her cases, plus doing horse activities...well, it's not like either of them had a ton of opportunity or time for a love life...and then there was the small fact that they were both cautious when it came to the opposite sex. How could they not be after watching their male cousins in action? Fuck 'em and forget 'em seemed to be the motto of the unmarried Maguire and Montgomery men.

"My lips are sealed," Cady said and Erin handed her the roll of film.

"Sorry I didn't have time to develop it. I just got in and I'm beat. It's bedtime for me."

A dark gray Chevy Dually pulled up in front of Cady's house. Erin grinned. "Looks like it's bedtime for you, too. I think this is my exit cue." But she lingered and watched as Kix unfolded himself from the truck. "Now if I could find someone like him, except maybe a school teacher instead of a lawman..." She leaned over and gave Cady a hug. "See you tomorrow. I won't bother saying sweet dreams—who needs 'em with a man like that around."

Cady's laugh followed Erin down the driveway.

Kix's heart expanded with pleasure at the sight of Cady. Damn, a man could get used to this—coming home to find his woman waiting for him, all soft and happy—though he figured her laughter probably came from something Erin had said, most likely about him showing up so late. But even that was heartwarming. He liked the way family was important to Cady. It was important to him. He didn't get around to see his brothers and parents as much as he'd like to, but it was a given in their family. Help was just a phone call away if anyone needed it.

Kix pulled Cady into a hug as soon as he got close enough. Damn, it felt good to hold her, to feel her body soften and mold itself to his.

She brushed a kiss against his mouth and he moaned, folding her in closer as his lips chased hers and demanded a more thorough greeting. When she whimpered, low and needy, his cock threatened to bust through his pants. Pulling back slightly, Kix whispered against her neck, "Darlin', maybe we better take this inside." When a wash of heat flooded her face, Kix felt an answering rush in the vicinity of his heart. Damned if she wasn't just plain adorable.

They made it to the living room before he tumbled her onto the couch and came down on top of her. His tongue went back to twining with hers while his hands worked the buttons of her shirt and released the front catch of her bra.

When his palms covered her breasts with their tight little pointed nipples, his pelvis jammed hard against hers in reaction. Panting, he raised himself so that he could look at what his hands were touching.

"Damn Cady, you've got the prettiest breasts. And your nipples..." He leaned down, licking over first one puckered areola, and then the other. "I could suck on them all day and still not get near enough."

Cady shivered and arched toward him, offering a glistening nipple and Kix groaned, latching on, sucking and tonguing the sensitive nub until she was whimpering and writhing underneath him, feverishly clawing at their clothing in an effort to feel skin on skin.

Ice-hot desire whipped down Kix's spine and more blood pulsed into his cock as his zipper gave and her hands slid into his jockeys. "Oh god, darlin', keep that up and I'm not going to be responsible for what happens," he panted when she cupped his balls with one hand and pumped his shaft with the other.

His penis grew harder and wetter in her hand and he shivered as feverish need built until the only thought in his mind was to put her on her hands and knees and take her like a stallion takes his mare.

"Darlin'," he groaned against her breast, "I've got to get inside you pretty damn quick here or I'm going to go all over your hot little cunt."

When his hand moved toward his back pocket, she stilled it with hers. He lifted his head and saw the delicate blush wash across her face. "I'm on the Pill," she whispered and his cock just about leaped out of her hand at the thought of plowing into her wet, tight sheath with no barriers between them.

"Damn Cady, you're just about to unman me." He got to his feet and scrambled out of his clothes, the thought of flesh-in-flesh making his cock leak and ache and need like it had never done before.

He forced himself to hold off, to help her get the rest of her clothes off and then buried his face between her legs, pressing his tongue in and out of her swollen slit until she came. Only then did he maneuver her off the couch, positioning her so that her pretty little backside was in the air, her legs spread and the plump folds of her cunt swollen and open for him.

Kix covered her then, sheathing his cock in her tight, wet channel in one powerful movement. She cried out, tightening like a fist around his hard flesh and wringing an answering sound for him.

Damn. He wasn't sure he could last more than a couple of strokes.

"Don't move, darlin'," he groaned against her soft, feminine shoulder.

The walls of her cunt gripped him even harder in response and he was lost. Unable to stop himself, he pumped in and out of her, bracing himself against the pleasure and the overwhelming need to press against her cervix and shoot his seed into her womb.

She whimpered and pleaded with her body, angling herself so that he went deeper with each thrust.

Kix licked and sucked along her neck, fighting against the urge to hold her in place the same way a stallion controls his mate, until finally he lost the battle and bit down on her smooth shoulder. She softened under him, growing even more submissive, and his hand moved around to her clit, squeezing and stroking until she cried out, her inner muscles clamping on his shaft seconds before fire ripped down his spine, pulling his balls tight, before raging through his cock in a release that left his ears ringing.

Chapter Seven

"Ten-to-one, there's cocaine in the box," Lyric said as she and Cady compared the photo Erin had taken to the photo Cady had taken on the backstretch of Angel Valdez talking to his agent.

"That's a leap."

Lyric shrugged. "Hey, it looks like a drug deal to me. How else do you explain what's going down in Erin's photo? Can you think of another reason why a horseracing protestor and a jockey would get together and pass something off?"

Cady couldn't, and that was frustrating. "Okay, so if we assume it's a drug deal and it's coke, then I guess we have to also assume that either, A—Valdez is hooked and buying it for himself, or B—he's planning on drugging more horses, which would make zero sense. First of all, it's possible that he actually rides for Adrienne, and second, even if he doesn't, why ruin her just because Terry beat him in a fistfight? Why not try and ruin Terry instead?"

"Who knows? The motive only has to make sense to the person committing the crime." Lyric grinned. "Damn, I wish I could have seen the fight. Then I'd know a little bit more about Valdez's style."

"Believe me, you would not like to hang around with Terry McKay."

"Don't need to be best friends with someone to enjoy seeing them go one-on-one."

Cady rolled her eyes. Thank God Kieran was on the scene now. Until he'd come along, both she and Erin had spent a lot of time worrying that one day their baby sister was going to stray a little too far on the wild side. "I've got to check this out. You're probably right about it being a drug deal, but it could have nothing to do with the track or what happened to Adrienne's horses. It could be that the track is just where Danny and Valdez first connected. Maybe protesting at the track is Danny's cover for building a new client base for the coke. From what Erin said, the Danny that got hauled away by the cops at the anti-fur demonstration didn't sound anything like the one I saw. If the police got called to Bay Downs, it would be because the protesters were loitering and doing nothing."

"You've got Danny's address on one of your release forms, right?"

"Yeah."

"So confront him with the photos and see what shakes out."

Cady's stomach tightened. She was better at observation and questions rather than direct confrontation. Maybe Kix...

As though reading Cady's mind, Lyric said, "Don't even go there. Use Kix as the 'big gun'," her eyebrows went up and down, "which, from the mouth-watering erection he usually sports when you're around, is probably an understatement. So I'll rephrase—use him as your cannon. If you don't get anything from Danny, let Kix flash his badge and try and persuade him. Same is true with Valdez."

Cady thought it over. She *was* the lead for the Crime Tells investigation. Bulldog would expect her to follow up on this and not turn it over to someone else—well, with the exception of her male cousins. And besides that, Kix was off to places unknown…

Okay, true, it's not like they'd talked much about the case last night…and somehow he'd managed—her entire body flushed when she remembered exactly how—to escape without telling her if his trip to San Francisco with Adrienne had led to any new leads. So she didn't owe him a call now that they had a hot lead.

Cady stiffened her resolve to not blur the line between her relationship with Kix and her responsibility as lead detective for Crime Tells. "I'll tackle Danny at work."

Lyric nodded. "That should be safe enough. I've got some running around to do for a new case. Promise you'll call if he's not at work and you end up going to his house."

"I'll give you a call." And since Cady hadn't heard about a new case coming in, she said, "A Crime Tells case or one of your own?"

"My own. A kid's pet tarantula is loose in a house over in Saratoga and they've got a fancy dinner party planned. According to the mother's social secretary, the party is major-league important, they offered me double my rates if I can find the thing before noon tomorrow when the caterers start showing up."

Cady laughed. Shane, Braden, and Cole always rolled their eyes at Lyric's "pet detective" sideline—but Cady was proud of her sister. "You'll find it."

"The question is—will I find it before someone sees it and faints…or worse, steps on it."

* * * * *

Second thoughts arrived as soon as Cady pulled into the animal control parking lot. She'd only been to the shelter once before, when a friend wanted to adopt a kitten. Once had been more than enough.

They'd gone at the height of the kitten season and there'd been a line of people waiting to surrender their *surplus* animals. Cady shuddered at the euphemism. That day the line had started at a counter somewhere in the building, then extended out the door and around the corner.

Even now the memory made Cady sick to her stomach. It didn't take a genius to figure out that very few of the kittens would find homes.

Cady took a deep breath and forced herself to go inside. She didn't see Danny at any of the front desks, or in the pet supply store. There were stairs leading to the management offices, but somehow she couldn't picture him in that role. That left the kennel area. Bracing herself, Cady pushed through the door leading to where the dogs were housed and immediately wished she'd decided to try Danny's house first.

The shelter was packed with dogs. There were three or four per cage and it seemed like all of them rushed to the front, barking and wagging their tails—trying to convince Cady to bail them out.

Okay, you can handle this. But she knew she couldn't as she moved through the rows of kennels, the images of their hopeful faces burning into her memory—a photographer's curse and blessing. Long after she left the shelter, she'd see these dogs in her mind's eye and wonder which ones found homes and which ones didn't.

One more row, then I'm home free. Just don't pet any of them and do not look any of them in the eye. You managed not to adopt a dachshund when Lyric ended up with almost two hundred of them. Cady's stomach roiled. *Of course, those dogs weren't at risk of being destroyed like these dogs are.*

She made it to the last kennel of the final row before her resolve failed. Then she was lost.

A huge, almost solid black, German shepherd caught her eye and Cady knelt down in front of him, pushing her fingers through the mesh of his kennel and rubbing one of his tall, elegant ears. He held steady, his piercing golden eyes focused on her face. She stroked him a few minutes longer, then shifted her attention to the card attached to his cage.

"So your name is Ranger, you're five years old and you were surrendered by your owner." A thick yellow line from a highlighter slashed across the front of the card.

Just as Cady was wondering about the yellow line, a young Hispanic woman approached. She had a blue nylon slip-lead in her hand. When she stopped in front of Ranger's run, Cady stood. "He's been adopted?"

The woman tapped a long red fingernail against the card, right where the yellow highlighter had made its pass. "ER."

"ER?"

"Euthanasia room." She tapped the red fingernail against the section on the card that listed the dog's age. "There's nobody going to want an old dog, especially a big one and we need the kennel space."

A tight fist of pain hit Cady's heart. "Five isn't old."

"It is here." The woman pulled a key out of her pocket and started to unlock the kennel.

"I'll adopt him."

The kennel attendant hesitated, shrugged, then pulled a pen from her pocket and scribbled "PA" on the card. Before Cady could ask, she said, "Potential adopter. That way no one will pull him and take him to the ER while you're filling out the paperwork. But it won't hold him for long."

Cady gave her a grateful smile even though her heart was pounding and a tap dance was going on in her stomach. "Where do I go?" *What have I done!*

"There are some forms on a rack right next to the front door. Anybody behind the desk can help you."

Cady thanked her, then numbly walked back in the direction she'd come from. Okay, what's the worst thing that can happen? Visions of leg-lifting and chewed-up furniture crossed her mind. *Okay, let's not go there. This'll work out. I'm a pet photographer. I know about pets and what I don't know, I can learn. And besides that, I'm not alone in this. Lyric and Erin will pitch in. They have dogs. Heck, almost everybody in our family has a dachshund now. Not that it's the same as a huge German shepherd, but...*

Within a few minutes of filling out a form and handing it to a woman behind the adoption desk, a tall black man stepped out from behind a partition and called Cady's name. He introduced himself as Marcus and led Cady to his workstation. It took only a minute to go over the paperwork. When Cady gave him a check, true panic threatened to set in. Since Ranger was already neutered, she was expected to take him with her—now.

"I don't even have a collar and leash," she blurted out the first thing that came to mind.

"We send the dogs out with one of those throwaway slip leads, but you're better off stopping in at our pet supply store and getting a real collar and leash. You're going to need one anyway." He glanced down at the paperwork. "Ranger weighs in at one-fifty, I'd definitely recommend a collar and a real leash. He's a lot of dog."

Marcus stood, forcing Cady to stand, too—and face the reality of what she'd just done. "Tell you what," he said, "it's slow enough that I can help you out."

Cady smiled in appreciation and followed him into the pet supply area. She picked out a hunter green collar with a matching leash and paid for them. Marcus took a few extra collars, just in case the one she'd chosen wasn't the right size.

As he escorted Cady back to the kennel she thought about the mission that had brought her to the shelter in the first place and said, "I met someone who works here, a guy named Danny Meyers. He was protesting at Bay Downs. But I don't see him here today."

Marcus shook his head. "Danny's in some big trouble. He didn't show for work yesterday and he's not here today either. The boss is pretty pissed. She usually cuts him some slack since he gets out and protests the causes she's into. But he didn't call in. That's a big no-no."

Cady thought about Erin's picture catching Danny as he scored a direct hit on the fur coat with his red paint. "Maybe he got arrested."

Marcus shrugged. "He gets arrested all the time. Couple of hours processing time and they kick him free. The jails are too full to hold demonstrators."

"Oh." They stopped in front of the kennel housing Cady's new dog. He stared at her again with those piercing golden eyes, then swished his tail. It was a subtle movement, not an exuberant display, but it shot like an arrow straight to Cady's heart.

This was going to work just fine. Hey, he'd be good company. Cady smiled as she envisioned Ranger riding around in the cab of the pickup with her. He was big enough, and scary enough, she wouldn't have to worry about anyone breaking in to steal her equipment.

Marcus unlocked the kennel and they stepped in. The collar Cady had selected fit perfectly. When she clipped the leash to it, Marcus said, "Looks like you're all set. Good luck with him."

"Thanks. I think it's going to be okay."

With each passing moment she felt more confident that she'd done the right thing. Ranger was perfect for her.

Despite dogs charging up to the front of their kennels and barking at him, he didn't react. He walked with regal dignity next to Cady, and even sat automatically when they stopped at her trunk.

She opened the door and started to tell him to jump in, but then thought better of it. Now that they were out of the shelter and one-on-one, there was no escaping the fact that her new companion stunk.

"I'll make it up to you," Cady promised as she walked around to the back of the truck, opening the door of the camper shell, then dropping the tailgate. Ranger jumped in without protest.

Cady made sure it was secure before climbing into the cab and reaching for her cell phone. Her heart kicked up a beat when she saw that Kix had called. For a second she looked at the phone and nibbled on her bottom lip, wondering if she should call and tell him about Danny not showing up for work—but then thought about her earlier decision and called Lyric. "Guess what, Danny's a no-show at work."

"Might still be in jail."

"That's what I thought. His coworker said Danny gets arrested all the time, but usually is out as soon as they process him."

"Could be true. California jails might as well have 'no vacancy' signs posted on them. So are you heading to his house now?"

Cady looked in her rearview mirror and saw Ranger. Lyric would find out about him soon enough. "It'll take me thirty or forty minutes before I can get there."

"Make it forty-five and I'll see you there."

"Okay." She gave Lyric the address and hung up.

Cady retrieved her appointment book and flipped to the back where she kept names and numbers. One advantage of being a pet photographer was that she knew a lot of people in the pet care industry. Within minutes she had an appointment for Ranger. While he was getting a bath, she and Lyric would hopefully be getting some answers from Danny Meyers.

* * * * *

"This looks like the VW in Erin's picture," Lyric said a few minutes later when she joined Cady. Her nose wrinkled. "Nice location. How long have you been here?"

"Just a few minutes." Cady looked up and down the street. Most of the houses had bars on the windows and junker cars in the front yard. Definitely not the kind of place she wanted to hang out in. Stinky or not, she'd been sorry she'd dropped Ranger off at the groomer's when she'd first gotten here.

"Ready?" Lyric asked.

"Yeah. Let's do it."

They dodged clumps of weeds sprouting through cracks in the sidewalk. A couple of yellowed newspapers lay in front of the door while the doorbell was popped out and hanging by a wire. Another frayed and broken wire jutted out of the hole where the bell had been attached.

"Nice," Lyric said again.

Cady gave the door a few good knocks.

The house remained quiet. No sounds. No movement.

She rapped again, even harder. "I don't hear anything. What about you?"

"No. Around back?"

Cady's blood started pounding in her ears at the thought of skulking around in this neighborhood.

Lyric grinned. "Don't worry, seeing people sneaking around will seem like normal behavior around here."

There was no way Cady could back down. Whether she went or not, Lyric would go. Her sister was a lot more pragmatic, and where Erin and Cady both had a finely tuned sense of self-preservation, Lyric didn't always give the impression that risk concerned her. Still, Cady felt compelled to say, "Okay, but no breaking and entering." Lyric snickered and headed around the house.

A rank smell greeted them at the side of the house near the garbage cans. The backyard was a disaster area with junked cars and weeds well past their knees. Cady noticed a rat sitting on top of the half-rotted wooden fence. It didn't even bother to hide when it saw them.

They waded through the weeds and knocked on the back door. Again no answer. The window in the door was covered with a gauzy type of curtain. Cady pressed her face as close to the glass as she could without actually touching anything.

There was a kitchen sink and a series of cabinets straight ahead. Cady moved further to the left in order to get more of a view. When she did, a hand and forearm came into sight and her heart stopped for a second. She took a quick step back, then moved forward again. The hand and forearm were on the table. Her view didn't let her see the person they were attached to. She stepped back again. "Someone's in there."

Lyric moved in and looked through the window, then pounded on the door. "Passed out maybe. He didn't even flinch. There's a window above the trash cans."

Cady knocked again, knowing where this was heading and wanting to head off an arrest for trespass. But Lyric was right, the arm on the table didn't move.

They retraced their steps to the side of the house. This time Cady noticed that the window above the trash cans was cracked open just a few inches. The stench was incredible and warning bells began shrieking in her head, especially when she noticed a steady stream of flies filtering in and out of the kitchen through a small hole in the screen. But she forced herself to gingerly climb onto the trash cans and peek in through the window.

The hand and forearm belonged to Danny all right. But from the looks of him, he wasn't going to need them — at least not in this lifetime.

Chapter Eight

"He's dead," Cady said, grimacing at the squeak in her voice. It wasn't like she hadn't seen plenty of dead bodies in her lifetime—but they'd always been where she expected to see them—not like this one.

Danny was sitting in a chair, but his upper body was lying on the kitchen table. His arms were spread out on either side. As far as she could tell, there was no obvious wound, no bullet hole, no blood splattered across the kitchen floor.

"Shit! Gunshot wound?" Lyric asked.

"There's no blood."

"Get down, let me see."

Cady was more than happy to relinquish her position on top of the trash can. Lyric scrambled up. "Shit, no wonder these flies are streaming through the window." She climbed off the can. "Okay, two choices, Cady. You can stay here while I go check the back door and see if it's open, and it will be, or you can come with me. But we've got to make our move now. As soon as we're inside, one of us has got to call the police. If some neighbor sees us go in, we don't want the cops asking why it took us five minutes to dial 911."

Cady closed her eyes briefly, not sure she wanted to see her sister in action, yet at the same time, she'd never been one to dodge the truth. On a sigh, she said, "Let's go," and Lyric's grin made her think of a kid who'd just been given free rein in the toy store.

They stopped in front of the back door. Lyric said, "Okay, once you're inside, pay attention to what you touch. If it's something that makes sense—like the phone, then handle it since it'd be suspicious if it was wiped clean. If it's something that wouldn't make sense, then be sure not to leave fingerprints."

Cady nodded. The thought of searching Danny's house while flies were swarming around his body made her feel a little queasy. True, he was dead and it didn't matter to him, while getting her reputation and career back *did* matter to Adrienne, but still…

Lyric pulled out a ring of keys, then bent over and studied the lockset before selecting a key and slipping it in. With a twist of her hand, the door unlocked. She straightened and grinned when she saw the expression on Cady's face. "Master keys. Braden took them off a poker player in Vegas last week. The guy's other line of work is burglary." She started to open the door, then paused, "When the police ask, the door was unlocked. Right?"

Cady gave a heartfelt sigh. "Right."

Lyric swung the door open and they both gagged, quickly covering their noses and mouths with their arms. If the smell near the side window was bad, the stench in the kitchen was a hundred times worse.

With the door open, Cady could see something she hadn't seen before—a syringe and a small plastic baggie with white powder in it just inches away from Danny's face. "You see that, Lyric? Looks like you were right."

They both moved over to the table. "Yeah, it looks like cocaine," Lyric said. "The cops may buy this as an overdose, but I don't."

Cady nodded slowly. "I'll ask Kix how often he's heard of someone shooting up with cocaine. And you can run it by Kieran." She looked up and spotted a phone hanging next to the kitchen door. "I'd better call 911."

"I'll start searching."

Cady made the call then searched the kitchen before moving to the living room. It was small, cluttered with books on animal rights and vegetarian cooking, and didn't hold any hint of a connection between Danny, Valdez, and the cocaine. The second bedroom had been converted to a weight and exercise room. Cady paused at the doorway just long enough to determine there was nothing of interest before joining Lyric in Danny's bedroom.

"Winner takes the pot with a Straight Flush," Lyric said and Cady moved to where her sister stood over an open dresser drawer. Inside were five little boxes identical to the one Erin's photograph had captured Danny handing off to Angel Valdez.

Her heart thundering in her throat, Cady carefully opened them one by one.

The first box had a small bag of the white powder. The next three were empty. The fifth contained a wad of bills.

"Looks like he was dealing." Cady carefully closed the boxes and pushed the dresser drawer in.

Lyric's eyebrows drew together. "Sure looks that way. I haven't found any syringes, what about you?"

Cady shook her head. "Nothing in the kitchen, living room, or weight room. I didn't hit the bathroom. Did you?"

"No." She used her thumb to point to the other side of Danny's bed. "I've checked everything else in here but the nightstand. I'll take a look in the bathroom, then head outside. Better hurry, a cop car could be rolling in any minute now."

Cady hustled over to the nightstand. She tried the single drawer first—condoms. Beneath, in the cabinet section, porn mags in neat stacks. There were some anti-fur pamphlets scattered on the top of the nightstand. The corner of a thin notebook caught her eye as she started to turn away. She sifted through the pamphlets and found an appointment book.

Cady opened it and wanted to do a little victory dance. Saturdays and Sundays for the last several weeks had *BD protest* scribbled on them. BD, Bay Downs. There was a brief notation, "anti-fur demo, SF" on the day Erin had seen Danny arrested for spraying paint on the fur coat. Cady slipped the appointment book into her pocket and rushed out of the house.

"Anything?" Lyric asked.

"An appointment book."

Lyric gave two thumbs up. "Please tell me you have it on you."

Cady nodded. "Any syringes in the bathroom?"

"Nope. And I'll bet there weren't any in the nightstand."

"Porn mags, condoms, and anti-fur pamphlets, plus the appointment book."

A police car showed up and a burly cop with an I-don't-take-shit-from-no-one attitude got out. He walked toward them with his hand on the butt of his gun and Cady had a bad feeling that she looked guilty as hell. It didn't help that Danny's appointment book felt like it was burning a hole through her pocket.

The cop zeroed in on her. "You call 911?"

Cady nodded.

"Where's the victim?"

"In the kitchen."

The cop grunted. "Let's see."

They led him around to the back. "Jesus," he said as soon as he got a whiff of the smell and saw the body generating it. "This guy a friend of yours?"

"No." Cady buried her hands in her pockets, which only exacerbated her awareness of the appointment book. She figured the less said, the better.

"Jesus," the cop muttered again before speaking into the radio attached to his collar. He moved into the kitchen and looked down at the table. "I'll be goddamned. Thirty years on the force, this is the first time I've seen somebody whack themselves this way."

Cady and Lyric exchanged glances. Cady feigned ignorance. "What's in the baggie?"

"Coke." The cop shook his head. "Don't see many users do it this way. Most are happy enough to run it through their nose or stupid enough to go for crack. Hell, since ecstasy hit the streets and heroin made a comeback, we don't see much of this stuff in this neighborhood anymore."

Another cop stomped around the side of the house, cursing and covering his nose and mouth as he rounded the corner. He paused when he saw Cady and Lyric in the doorway. "You in there, Minelli?"

"Yeah. Looks like an OD. Go ahead and call it in. Tell 'em he's been here for awhile and he's pretty ripe."

Minelli turned back toward Cady and Lyric. "Let's go around to my car."

Cady's heart did a racing circuit down to her stomach and up through her ears as they followed him around front. *Okay, take a deep breath here. There are absolutely no grounds for him to do a search and find the appointment book.*

Minelli pulled a clipboard from his patrol car. "So how did you ladies come to find the body?"

Cady decided to stick close to the truth. "We wanted to ask him some questions about a case we're working on."

Minelli squinted. "Let's see some ID." They produced it. Minelli grunted. "You related to Bulldog Montgomery?"

"His granddaughters," Cady said.

Minelli's eyes narrowed. "Didn't know Bulldog handled cases involving drugs."

The silence hung heavily between them. Cady knew he wanted her to fill it with information, she bit her lip to keep from saying anything. He grunted again. "The body has been in there for awhile, you see anything suspicious?"

"No," Cady said.

Minelli turned to Lyric. "You?"

"No—except for the smell and the flies. That's what made us look through the side window and check the back door."

Minelli tapped his pen on the clipboard, then came to some kind of silent decision. "Okay, you're free to go. We need you for anything, we know where to find you."

Cady and Lyric started to turn. He said, "Tell me something. Most women come across a scene like that one and they're in hysterics. Didn't seem to bother you two any. How come?"

Cady relaxed. "Our other grandfather embalmed people for a living. When Bulldog wasn't around to baby-sit, we ended up hanging out at the funeral home with Grandpa Maguire. We've spent a lot of time playing hide-and-seek and wandering into rooms we shouldn't have."

Minelli grunted and nodded. Lyric and Cady returned to their cars.

"You heading home?" Cady asked.

"No. I'm going to Erin's house. What about you?"

Cady grinned, thinking about her new dog. She could hardly wait for her sisters to see Ranger. "I've got a stop to make first, then I'll be home."

Lyric's eyebrows went up. "From the look on your face, does your stop involve a 'quickie' with Kix?"

Cady laughed and opened her truck door. "Nope. But you'll find out about it in a little while."

* * * * *

Lyric almost kept driving when she saw her husband's Harley parked in front of Erin's house. Damn! She should have known Minelli would call Kieran as soon as she and Cady drove away from Danny Meyers' house.

That was so like cops, to stick together. And it didn't help that Kieran was a vice cop and Danny's vice was coke. Shit! She dug around in her pocket and retrieved the set of master keys, then tossed them under her car seat. She could *not* let Kieran find those! He'd be compelled to confiscate them and then she'd never hear the end of it from Braden. Already her cousin got a huge kick out of joking about how Kieran had tamed her. Oh yeah, she could hardly wait for the day when Braden met his match. He'd find out that it could be a hell of a lot more fun to push the limits at home where the difference between punishment and reward could be deliciously blurred, than it was to always test the rules on the outside.

Lyric's cunt tightened and sent a rush of liquid to her panties just thinking about Kieran's various punishments. Oh yeah, bring 'em on.

She parked in front of her sister's house and groaned when Kix's gleaming 4x4 pulled up behind the Jeep. Damn. Uniformed cop to vice cop to sheriff—didn't interesting news travel fast.

She should have waited until Cady got here before telling Erin anything. Instead she'd brought Erin up to date on the case and told her what they'd found at Danny's house when she called to tell her sister she was on her way over. Not a good move. No doubt Erin had felt duty-bound to fill Kieran in when he called.

Lyric checked her cell phone, no messages. Tricky. Her husband knew Erin would tell him anything he wanted to know and give him the ammunition he needed. She shook her head. Even though Erin had only stayed on the police force for a year, she was still pretty much devoted to law and order. Their cousin Cole was the same way. It probably had something to do with being the oldest kid in each of their families. Lyric sighed. It was a major bummer sometimes.

Bulldog wasn't territorial about sharing information with the law as long as it served Crime Tells' and the client's interests. Still…Lyric hoped that Erin had drawn the line when it came to disclosing the little tidbit of information about Danny's appointment book ending up in Cady's back pocket.

Kieran stepped out of Erin's house and Lyric's heart went triple-time at the sight of his dark expression and his equally fierce hard-on. Oh yeah, bring it on. She'd bet her own Harley that she wasn't going to be here when Cady got home.

* * * * *

Kix stood in masculine glory on Cady's front steps, hands on his hips, scowl on his face, erection pressed against the front of his faded jeans, and Cady's heart started tap-dancing in her chest. No wonder Lyric always anticipated getting home when Kieran was hot and bothered and waiting for her! Wow!

"Darlin', I've already heard an abbreviated version of what you and Lyric were up to and you can bet that pretty little ass of yours that we're going to have a talk about it," he said as she climbed out of her truck.

"We can talk, but I have to get Ranger settled in first." She stepped to the side and let the dog jump out.

Kix's expression went from scowl to bemusement. "You got a dog?"

"They were going to put him to sleep."

"You got a dog." This time there was amusement in his voice.

"Yes, I did."

The lazy grin spread across his face and she knew she was in trouble when he did his loose-hipped cowboy saunter down the walkway.

"Little darlin', did you set out to get a dog this morning?"

"I'm going to take the Fifth," she muttered.

"Hmmm, now there's a challenge." His smile widened and Cady thought he was going to lean forward and kiss her. Instead he held his hand out for Ranger to sniff. The dog's tail gave an almost imperceptible wag.

"He likes you," Cady said.

"Dogs and women both find me irresistible."

Cady rolled her eyes. "Maybe you could make yourself useful and carry in the dog bed and his food."

Kix chuckled before moving closer and pulling her up against his body, giving her the kiss she'd been expecting. When it ended, he rubbed his nose along hers before resting his forehead on Cady's. "Don't think we're not going to have a little chat about you haring off on your own to confront a suspect."

"I was hardly on my own. Lyric was with me."

"Well, judging from the things Kieran had to say, that might be even worse than going alone. I have a sneaking suspicion you wouldn't have ventured into Danny's house if your sister wasn't along."

"You talked to Kieran?"

"Oh yeah, darlin', we had a nice long talk about the Montgomery streak of independence and way of doing things. You want to know what we do with pretty little law breakers in my county?" Despite the teasing edge to his words, his body told a different story.

She snorted. "I'm not a law breaker."

"Breaking and entering, trespass..." When she tensed, he pulled back and studied her face.

Cady cursed herself for thinking about the appointment book in her back pocket and stiffening. To cover, she said, "It was hardly breaking, entering, and trespassing. The door was unlocked when Lyric tried it. And then seeing Danny like that... I think that's called probable cause to enter."

He laughed. "Oh, Kieran was pretty sure that the door would be unlocked. Funny thing, the doors are always unlocked when Lyric's on the scene. Your sister is in for a very thorough body search."

Cady snickered. "Oh yeah, and Lyric'll enjoy every second of it." She just hoped that Lyric had time to hide the keys. She'd feel guilty if Lyric lost her new toys because she helped out today.

Ranger nudged Cady's hand. "I've got to take him inside and get him settled."

Kix pressed a hard kiss against her lips. "We're not finished with this discussion. There's a tingling at the back of my neck that I've learned to listen to. And the funny thing is, darlin', it started when Erin quit talking right on the verge of telling Kieran and me just what you and Lyric found while you were being such good citizens and waiting for the police to show up."

Chapter Nine

The truce lasted long enough for Cady to feed Ranger and let him investigate the backyard before checking out the rest of the house and finally laying down on the dog bed she put in front of the TV. The moment he was settled, Kix moved into Cady's personal space and said, "Now, am I going to have to frisk you, then handcuff you, or are you planning to cooperate?"

Cady nibbled on her bottom lip.

"Darlin', I'm just barely under control here."

"That's not my problem."

"Well now, Cady, I think you're wrong about it not being your problem." Kix pulled her back tight against the front of his body and teased her with the feel of his lips along her neck.

She shivered but didn't back down from what had been on her mind. "You haven't exactly been keeping me up-to-date on what you're doing."

His chuckle had Cady closing her eyes and thinking about the way smooth, warm chocolate could slide down and heat you from the inside out.

Kix slid his hands up and started unbuttoning her shirt. "I'm willing to show you mine if you're willing to show me yours."

She gave in for a second, enjoying his touch, his teasing, but then regret forced its way in. Cady stiffened and tried to pull away from him. She wasn't immune to him, but that didn't mean that she was going to keep letting him use her... No she wasn't going to go there, that was unfair to both of them... She wasn't going to let him use his charm to sidestep the fact that so far the sharing of case information seemed to only go one way.

When he didn't release her, she stopped struggling and said, "Please let me go, Kix."

He stepped back but kept his hands on her arms, turning her so that they faced each other. Sure enough, something was going through his little darlin's mind and he had a bad feeling that if he didn't head it off, he was going to end up in a world of hurt.

He felt like a dog that was one step away from being hit with a rolled-up newspaper and sent out to the doghouse, but that didn't stop him from stiffening his spine and asking the question no man likes to ask his woman. "What's wrong?"

The silence stretched out like a tight leash and Kix was just about to open his mouth and ask again when Cady said, "Did you really mean it? About sharing your information? I don't have a clue what you've found out so far...which is okay if we're working separately and this..." she blushed and waved her hand between them "...and this is something else altogether..." She stood a little straighter. "I'm fine with us doing our own thing and still seeing each other outside of the case. I mean, you're working for Adrienne and Crime Tells is working for Alex." She took a deep breath. "I just need to know where the lines are so I don't end up feeling...bad when it's over."

For a second Kix felt poleaxed. Was she talking about the case being over or them being over? And was his little darlin' implying that she wondered if he was using her? Pain ripped through Kix—followed by resolve.

Damned if he didn't know exactly how to deal with this. You dealt with it the same way you did when a horse spooked and threw you. You got back on and rode 'till it knew it could trust you.

He pulled Cady flush against his body and gave her a fierce kiss before stepping away. "Hang on, darlin', I've got to get something from the truck before we can finish this conversation."

Cady watched him stride away, nervous shivers racing along her spine as her heart rate accelerated. Something about his purposeful movement set off warning bells and made her almost sorry that she'd voiced her doubts, but dammit…when it came to relationships she didn't know any other way except to just lay her cards on the table.

He was gone for several long, slow moments. When he returned he took Cady's arm and silently led her to the bedroom door, only pausing long enough to look at the German shepherd and say, "Stay there, partner," before ushering her inside and closing the door behind them.

"Darlin', it cuts me to the quick that you don't trust me…"

Cady opened her mouth only to have him shake his head and cover her lips with his long enough to stop her. "Don't say anything, don't deny it. Deep down, that's what's going on here, and I aim to fix it right now."

An edge of fear skittered along her spine when he pulled four strips of leather out of his back pockets and tossed them on the bed. When he started to unbutton her shirt, Cady felt like her heart was planning on jumping out of her chest and making a run for it. Her cunt on the other hand… She shivered, closing her legs in an effort to appease the ache centered in her clit, the need that had her lower lips swollen and parted, wet with anticipation. Hadn't she always fantasized about a man doing this to her?

Still, her survival instinct struggled to overwhelm her fantasies. She tried to pull back only to meet the steel resistance of his arm around her waist.

His face was a portrait of masculine determination as he removed her shirt and dropped it to the floor. She tensed, expecting the bra to follow, instead, he whispered a kiss across her chest, teasing along the border of soft fabric with his tongue and lips before brushing across her tight cloth-covered nipples. When she whimpered he raised his head and brought his face to hers so that their eyes could meet. "I'm only going to say this once, little darlin'—what I want from you doesn't have anything to do with Adrienne's problem, but it's got everything to do with what a man wants from his woman, including having her trust him." He gave her a hard kiss. "It seems like we've got a little trouble starting in that area, which I aim to head off right now."

Cady couldn't help shivering. "By tying me up?"

The dark look in his eyes was answer enough. He undid the front clasp of her bra, then reached for the snap of her jeans. Her hands moved to his shoulders, opening and closing on the material of his shirt as fear warred with anticipation. She wasn't sure that she could really go through with this, with being completely helpless.

"I believe you," she blurted out, "about not…about this being separate from the case."

A muscle twitched in his jaw. "I'm glad to hear that, little darlin'. If I haven't been telling you what I've been doing, it's because I haven't found anything worth calling your attention to, especially when you've been doing a damned fine job of looking into other things."

"Oh." She had a second of feeling guilty before her jeans slipped to her ankles and the trepidation returned full force. "I trust you. You don't need to…"

He silenced her again with a kiss. This one dark and dominating. "Darlin', unless you look me in the eye and tell me that you don't want this, then I'm not going to stop."

Cady's heart thundered in her ears, rushing in a primitive beat that pulsed through her body. Her mouth parted just enough for her teeth to worry her bottom lip.

When she didn't say anything, Kix's warm hands slid over her hips and down her legs, taking her panties with them. He knelt in front of her, removing her shoes and freeing her from her clothing.

A flush washed across Cady's face and breasts. Embarrassment meshed with anxiety and arousal at being naked while he remained clothed.

"Damn you're beautiful, Cady darlin'," Kix said as his hands curled around her legs, stroking upward until they moved around to cup her buttocks and pull her forward. "You were made for loving." Almost reverently he brushed his cheek against her pubic hair before nuzzling her swollen clit and labia.

Cady's heart soared. No one had ever made her feel like Kix did.

His tongue washed over her clit before stroking into her slit. Cady whimpered in reaction and he thrust his tongue in deeper, making her knees go weak.

She grabbed his shoulders and his husky laugh sent more blood racing to her already swollen cunt. Kix sucked her clit quickly, then stood and pulled her against his body as he trailed kisses up her neck and around the shell of her ear. "A man could get mighty distracted down there." His fingers traced along her spine. "Now get on the bed darlin'."

Cady shivered at the command, at the images that assailed her. "Are you going to get undressed first?"

Kix pressed his jeans-covered leg between her thighs, heightening her feelings of vulnerability as his tongue explored her ear further, flicking in and out and making her breasts feel heavy and tight. "No, darlin', now get on the bed or you're going to feel my hand on your backside."

Cady's stomach clenched as he released her. The air shuddered in and out of her lungs as she stepped backward, coming to a halt when she touched the bed. Out of the corner of her eye she could see the thin strips of leather on the hunter green comforter.

Her resolve weakened and she stood there for a long second. Kix moved forward and her eyes went immediately to his hands. "I can count to three if that's the way you want this to go." When she didn't get on the bed immediately, he took another step. "One, darlin'."

Cady's clit pulsed and she clamped her legs together tightly as arousal escaped past the lips of her cunt and coated her inner thighs.

Kix took another step and Cady was mesmerized by the hunger she saw in his face. "Two, darlin'."

Her eyes dropped to his heavy, cloth-covered erection and she sat down on the bed, knowing in that instant that when he gave her a spanking, she wanted to feel his hot flesh against hers. Kix took the last step and she slid backward so that she was sitting completely on the comforter. "You cut that pretty close," he whispered, gripping her knees and pulling her legs apart so that he could look at her.

His cock jumped at the sight of her slick, swollen flesh, at the way her inner thighs glistened, wet with her need. Damn, he was already hanging on to control by a thread and she was making it harder.

"Lay back, darlin' and put your hands over your head," he ordered.

Moisture leaked from the slit in his cock as she positioned herself on the bed, her breasts shaking, her breathing becoming more erratic. Kix reached down and gripped himself through the now-too-tight jeans as he fought the urge to free his penis and shove it into her welcoming heat.

He took a deep breath and forced his hand away from the front of his jeans. His cock felt like a gunfighter with a jumpy trigger finger. One wrong move and it was going to shoot. He reached for the ties and crawled onto the bed, gritting his teeth at being so close to Cady.

He bound her wrists to the bed first, then her ankles. The smell of her arousal swamped his senses while her show of trust flooded his heart with emotion.

For several long minutes, all he could do was look at her. Goddamn. Now he understood why his brother Jake kept saying he wanted to rope that woman he'd taken a fancy to and tie her to the bed.

Kix had never thought a whole lot about trying it before Cady came along. But damn... He liked knowing that her trust ran deep enough to allow him to see her like this...open and vulnerable, dependent on him for her pleasure.

He wasn't sure how long he was going to last, but one thing was for certain, he couldn't stand not feeling her skin against his own. He stood up long enough to shed his clothes, then covered her body with his body, groaning as his cock bathed in the arousal that coated her cunt lips and inner thighs.

His mouth found hers and she opened for him immediately, her pelvis arching upward in invitation. He bucked against her, his cock hungry and desperate to feel the tight fist of her sheath.

Kix groaned and pulled back from her mouth, biting and kissing down her neck until he reached her breasts. He used his hands to push the mounds together so that he could easily alternate between their hardened peaks.

Cady arched with each lick, and when he began sucking, her buttocks tightened and her hips jerked, driving her clit against his heavy erection. "Harder," she pleaded, so close to coming.

He settled more of his weight on her and moved his hips, rubbing along her swollen clit as he continued his assault on her breasts. He'd always been a breast man, and now that he'd been with Cady, he didn't figure another pair of them would ever turn him on like hers did. Damn if he couldn't bury his face in her soft flesh and stay there forever, suckling and biting and loving on her.

His cock jerked as her whimpers became more urgent. A warm flow of pre-cum escaped and he knew that he was running out of time. Groaning, Kix tore his attention from Cady's love-roughened nipples and returned to her lips, thrusting his tongue into her mouth just as his penis found the haven of her wet cunt.

She cried out, her taut body arching underneath him. He moved in and out of her forcefully, swallowing her sobs and cries until finally her inner muscles gripped him so tightly that he had to lift his head and shout as lava-hot seed and almost unbearable pleasure rushed through his cock.

He untied her then, somehow finding the energy to get them both under the covers before pulling her against his body so that her breasts pressed tightly against his chest. "Damn, darlin'," he whispered, his penis twitching in reaction to being so close to her slit, "I wanted to love you all over before riding you."

Cady twined her legs with his and snuggled into him. Her heart was still pounding and her nerve endings felt shivery from what had just happened between them. She wasn't sure if she could have stood any more. It had been intense…scary…unsettling…addictively erotic. "Maybe we'll save that for another time," she whispered against his damp flesh.

Kix buried his face in her wild curls and smiled in relief. Now that he'd had a taste of doing this with a woman—with *his* woman—he wanted to do it again, only next time she would scream in release more than once. Damn, he was crazy about her.

The silence settled around them as their bodies slowed and calmed. Cady trailed her fingers down his side, her thoughts returning to the case. "So exactly what have you been looking into?"

Kix rolled and pulled her on top of him. "Following up on the fact that eleven trainers have been suspended since the beginning of the year. Far as I can tell, at least six of them are probably guilty of trying to cheat. The rest of the them I don't know about yet."

Goose bumps washed over Cady's flesh as Kix traced a finger along her spine. "You ready to tell me just what you and Lyric found at Meyers' place?"

Chapter Ten

"An appointment book. The trouble is, he used abbreviations. And between picking Ranger up from the groomer's and finding you here, I haven't had time to figure out what any of them mean."

Kix's hand stilled at the back of her spine before moving lightly over her buttocks. "Am I hearing you right, darlin'? You took evidence from a crime scene?"

A cold knot of worry began to form in Cady's stomach. "It wasn't a crime scene. The cops were calling it an overdose."

Kix snorted. "It wasn't a crime scene yet. And you and Lyric already guessed that. As soon as the medical examiner does an autopsy, they'll be looking for a murderer. You can take that to the bank and deposit it." His hand settled on one ass cheek. "If I wasn't worn out from lovin' you, Cady, I'd sit up and spank your pretty little butt for doing something so crazy."

Cady shivered in reaction and her nipples went to tight points against Kix's hard chest. He tensed and she could feel his erection growing against her abdomen.

"You'd like that, wouldn't you, little darlin'?" He kissed and sucked his way up her neck before running his tongue around the shell of her ear. "You'd like to feel my hand against your backside."

"Maybe," she whispered, feeling the blood rush to her clit and labia. "Not necessarily now, but someday...I'd like to try it."

Kix closed his eyes against the wave of love and lust that poured through him. Damn, if she wasn't just plain perfect for him—the answer to a prayer he didn't even know he'd sent off. She was everything he could have asked for, and to know that she was opening up, trusting him in ways she'd never trusted another man, well, that left him just about as defenseless as a newborn calf. Goddamn if she hadn't managed to rope and hog-tie him faster than a cowboy doing a championship rodeo run.

He rolled her over and settled on top of her, groaning when her legs wrapped around his hips and his penis dipped into the wet, welcoming heat of her. "Damn Cady, you feel so good."

She pulled his head down. "You feel pretty good yourself, cowboy." She grinned and nibbled along his bottom lip before adding, "Or should I call you sheriff?"

"Well, darlin', if I was acting in my capacity as a law keeper, then your pretty backside would be feeling the sting of my hand." He began pumping in and out of her. "But right now my cock isn't willing to leave this little piece of heaven, so I think we'd better just settle in for a long slow cowboy's ride." He leaned down and gave her a leisurely kiss. "Make that a long slow ride with a beautiful view."

A blush washed across Cady's face as love battled with uncertainty in her chest. She was attractive, but she'd never considered herself beautiful, not when compared to Erin's stunning looks or Lyric's wild sensuousness.

"You're the one that's beautiful to look at," she blurted out, trying to hide her vulnerability. "And better than chocolate."

He laughed and brushed a kiss over her lips. "Better than chocolate. That sounds like mighty high praise."

"The highest."

He settled more heavily on her then, anchoring her body to the bed and changing the angle so that his cock stroked even deeper. She arched underneath him and tightened her grip.

Kix groaned at the way her slick tight muscles clamped down on him, trying to keep him buried inside her wet depths. He wanted to take it slow and easy, to luxuriate in the feel of her soft breasts against his chest, to savor every inch of her tight sheath and enjoy the way his balls slapped and rubbed against her skin, but damned if they weren't already pulling tight, warning him that he wasn't going to last near as long as he wanted to. Hell, the truth of the matter was that he wanted to park his cock in her pretty little cunt and never leave.

He stilled, trying to stave off his climax and Cady whimpered, "Oh god, Kix, please don't stop."

He covered her mouth with his as he slid his hand down, gently caressing her buttock before moving to explore the crevice between her ass cheeks. She tensed and sent a wave of pleasured agony through his cock and up his spine. Damn, she was already so tight…it'd be heaven and hell if she was any smaller.

Kix had to close his eyes as the thought of her wearing a butt plug worked its way into his thinking. Goddamn, where had that fantasy come from? He knew his brother liked to do that with his women — it was one of the things they had a blast teasing Walker about when they got together and played poker… Hell, that was just the tip of the iceberg when it came to what Walker liked. Kix had never figured that he wanted a lot of "extras"…but damned if his cock wasn't growing harder and hungrier at the thought of having to push into an even smaller, tighter space than the one it was already in.

His fingers circled and brushed across the pucker of her back entrance and she clamped down even harder on him. He moaned, knowing he wasn't going to be able to take much more before he'd have to start pumping again. He rose up so that he could see her face as he slipped just the tip of his juice-coated finger in her anus.

A flush washed against her face, embarrassment and unwilling arousal and his heart melted like chocolate left in the heat. "You want to know what I'm thinking, Cady?"

He slid the finger in a little further. "I'm thinking that one day I'd like to see you wearing a butt plug back here. I'd like to have to fight and struggle to get inside you. Would you do that for me, darlin'?"

The flush deepened and when she whispered "yes", her answer put him over the edge. Kix sealed his lips to hers, pressing his tongue into her mouth in the same rhythm as his hips surged against her, as his cock filled and caressed her tight channel.

He may have started out slow and easy, but the sounds she made, the way she clung to him and gave herself over to his loving, turned his gentle thrusts into a wild primitive need to mate that had him driving into her hard and fast and deep until she cried out, sending a flood of heat over the sensitive head of his penis. His lips left hers and a guttural shout was torn from him as wave after wave of icy-hot satisfaction whipped down his spine, tightening his balls before rushing through his cock in an explosion that left him panting and shaking above her.

Later they settled on the couch to go through Danny's appointment book. They started with the current week. Cady tapped the notation about protesting at Bay Downs on Sunday.

"This still bothers me, especially after what Erin saw." Her hand moved to the anti-fur protest scribbled in on Monday. "Lyric thinks that protesting at the race might have been a cover for selling the coke, but that doesn't make sense to me. For one thing, it's not like there was a crowd of likely buyers there. And for another, it's too out in the open, plus why have four other people hanging around." She thought about the pale blonde, who actually seemed passionate about the cause, and then the other three who acted like they were on a long break. "It's like a photograph that just doesn't come together correctly. The picture seems okay when you look at it quickly, but if you examine it closely, you see areas that are out of focus or taken from the wrong angle. A real protester would have tried to talk us out of going through the gate, but Danny didn't even have any pamphlets to give us, even though there were a lot of pamphlets on anti-fur and anti-factory farming in his house."

"You're right, it doesn't fit. And for the record, I don't think he was there to sell drugs. Too much work and too big an investment of time." Kix tapped the initials BAR that appeared on Sunday, Wednesday, Friday, and Saturday. "Ring any bells?"

Cady shook her head. "There's also no AV penciled in for Monday. But I guess that makes sense. Erin said that based on the way Danny was acting, she didn't think he was expecting Angel Valdez to show up at the protest."

Kix flipped backward. "Bay Downs and BAR were scheduled just like they were on the previous pages. Here's AV at nine p.m. on Tuesday."

"That's two days before the coke turned up in Adrienne's horses."

"Sure is, little darlin'." He flipped another page and a wave of dread washed through Cady when she saw the initials AFF. She shivered and Kix put an arm around her shoulders. "You cold?"

She touched the initials. "The Animal Freedom Front. Have you heard of them?"

"Sure have."

"Lyric dealt with them on a case she had." Cady thought about the scar on Lyric's side. A few inches over and the bullet would have killed her sister. "Kieran says he'd take on organized crime or wade into a gang war before he'd tangle with them—well, tangle with the cell Lyric had contact with. They scare me."

Kix pulled her against him. "I'm glad to hear that, darlin'. Now I won't have to worry about you haring off to investigate that angle. A little bit of fear can go a long way toward keeping a person alive and out of trouble."

She shivered again, then remembered the pamphlets she'd seen in Danny's house. "If he was in the AFF, I don't think he was in a cell that focused on horse racing. It looked like he was more interested in factory farming and animals being killed for their fur."

Kix nodded and they continued paging toward the front of the appointment book, encountering the same pattern of initials over and over again along with additional notations about protests, reminders of court dates and various times for working additional shifts at the animal shelters. At the beginning of each month, the letter B appeared. "You notice that when B appears, AV doesn't?" he asked.

"Yeah. Too bad we don't have more to go on. 'B' could be anyone or anywhere."

Kix got to the second page of the calendar before a new set of initials showed up. Two days after Danny had attended a banquet in honor of the donors, volunteers and staff who worked at the animal shelter, he'd noted in his appointment book, *10 p.m., BCC, San Francisco.*

"I think maybe I'd better photocopy this just in case we have to turn it over to the police," Cady said as Kix closed the appointment book.

Kix grunted. "Not if, darlin', when. You got a copier here?"

"In my office."

"Why don't you go and make a copy and I'll check in with Kieran."

Cady grimaced. The idea of Kix and Kieran collaborating did not set her mind at ease. True, Kieran had gotten better…slightly…but he still tended to think in caveman terms. The man handles the danger. The little woman stays out of it.

"I take it you two hit it off."

Kix gave her the slow cowboy grin that touched every part of Cady's insides and stroked over her erogenous zones. "Well, darlin', when it comes to our womenfolk, we hold pretty much identical views."

"That's what I was afraid of," Cady said as she stood and made her way to the small bedroom that she'd converted to an office.

Kix chuckled as he watched Cady move off. Damned if she didn't satisfy him all the way to the core. She was lively enough to keep him on his toes, but soft and gentle enough to make a man anxious to get home at night just to hold her. Kieran might have caught himself a beautiful, fiery handful when he managed to rope Lyric, but Kix didn't envy the vice cop that wild ride.

Kix dug out his cell phone and made the call. "Anything new?"

"The medical examiner has got the autopsy scheduled for tomorrow, sometime before noon. Right now they've got the case marked as a suspicious death, maybe a suicide. No obvious struggle marks on the body. But the word is that he was finally going to do some serious time. Turns out the lady whose coat he spray painted in San Francisco was the wife of some big deal politico."

"When will you have the autopsy results?"

"Don't know. I'll give you a call as soon as I know something. In the meantime, I've got a request in for a copy of his phone records."

"Great. Just a heads up, there's a stray piece of evidence that needs to get corralled if it turns into a murder investigation."

"Son of a bitch!"

"I take it your wife didn't mention the appointment book that followed the ladies home."

"I can't fucking believe it! She knows the rules about that!"

Kix nearly laughed out loud. Somehow he didn't think Cady's little sister stayed well-acquainted with rules for long stretches at a time. It'd be a challenge, but Kix intended to make sure those habits didn't rub off on Cady. "I'll keep you posted," he told Kieran before signing off. He paused long enough to make sure Cady was still in her office before dialing Adrienne and getting Valdez's address, along with confirmation that the jockey wasn't scheduled to race until the next night.

It was time to pay a little visit to Angel Valdez. Maybe Valdez seeing a badge and the picture of the coke hand-off was all it would take for this whole thing to be tied up neater than a cow in a roping event.

Cady returned a few minutes later, practically jumping through her skin with excitement. "BAR is Betty Anne Remmick! I stuck with the cover story that I'm a photographer. But I told her that you were a sheriff investigating some bad stuff at the track. I kept it vague. She's willing to talk to us right now!"

"Betty Anne Remmick?"

"The protester—the really pale blonde who gave me the pamphlet and actually seemed interested in their cause. When I went to file the photocopies I saw her release form and made the connection."

Kix uncurled from the couch, pulling her into his arms and giving her a quick kiss. "That's mighty fine detecting, darlin'. Let's head out and see if we can round up some information. "

Chapter Eleven

Cady felt a surge of sympathy for Betty Anne Remmick. Her pale white face was splotchy-red from a prolonged cry.

Betty Anne stepped back from the doorway, a long sniffle sounding as she pulled mucus back up into her nasal passages. "Come on in."

The place was a disaster, but not as a result of Betty Anne's bereavement. Bundles of leaflets lay everywhere. Dishes with particles of dried-on food littered just about any surface that wasn't already claimed by paper material or dirty clothes.

Betty pointed to a stained, grungy couch, and Cady wondered how awkward it would be to question her while sitting on Kix's lap, then thought better of it. Sitting on his knee would only make her think about sex and God knew it was hard to think about anything else when she was around him.

She sat on the edge of the sofa, taking up the least amount of space while getting a good view of a man's sock and a pair of underwear on the carpet beneath the coffee table.

Betty Anne gave another loud mucus-filled sniffle. "You calling was like the answer to a prayer. When I heard that Danny was dead, I went to the police department. They wouldn't tell me anything at first, and then they started asking me about whether I knew that Danny sold drugs. No way! He wasn't like that! Then they told me that he overdosed on cocaine. That's a lie! Danny didn't even drink sodas or go into fast-food places."

"Sometimes people can fool you," Kix said.

Betty Anne reached for a tissue and cleared her nasal passages. "Not Danny. He and I were like that." She held up her hand, the first two fingers pressed together. We've been together since the beginning of the year."

"How'd you meet Danny?" Cady asked.

Betty Anne sniffed again and then took a deep breath. "I met him at a rally. He was more animal rights than animal welfare, but we were attracted to each other." She gave Cady a woman-to-woman look. "You know how it is. Sometimes you see a guy and it all just clicks."

Cady shifted and ending up brushing against Kix. She nodded at Betty Anne.

"Well, it was like that for Danny and me. After the rally we went to his place and…you know. It was every bit as good as I thought it was going to be. From then on we started seeing each other every chance we got. It was like…like… I don't know how to explain it… Totally awesome. The best."

"Is that why Danny was doing the Bay Downs protest?" Cady asked. "Because of you?"

Betty Anne started fiddling with a pamphlet on the coffee table. "No. Bay Downs was his idea."

Cady still couldn't get that piece of the puzzle to fit. If protesting at the track was Danny's idea, why wasn't he inspired like he'd been at the anti-fur rally? "My sister saw Danny at the anti-fur protest in San Francisco."

Betty Anne blew her nose. "I wasn't there. But one of our friends told me what happened." Her eyes teared up again. "I had to work, maybe if I'd gone... Danny was one of the bravest guys I've ever met. He was willing to take a fall for a cause if he believed in it."

"Did you see him after he was arrested?" Kix asked.

Betty Anne shook her head. "Sunday was the last time I saw him. We came here after protesting at the track and hung out for the rest of the day."

"What got him interested in the horse races?" Kix asked and Betty Anne went back to fiddling with the pamphlet.

"I don't know. Danny was like that. He had lots of different animal causes that he was interested in."

"Will the rest of you keep protesting now that Danny's gone?" Cady asked.

"No. I'd like to. Once I learned about what happens to the horses, I wanted to do something. But it would just be me. The other three aren't going to come out anymore."

Cady leaned forward. "How come?"

Betty Anne went back to fiddling with the pamphlet again. This time she used her forefinger to hold it down and her thumb to spin it around and around. She shifted uncomfortably in her seat. Finally she sighed and asked, "This won't go into your book, will it?"

It took Cady a split second to remember the "A Day at the Track" book that the protestors had assumed she was working on. "What won't go into the book?"

"What I'm about to tell you."

"If you say it's off the record, I won't put it in."

Betty Anne spun the pamphlet again. "A lot of people don't feel comfortable protesting, and there are so many causes anyway. It's hard to get more than a few people, especially on weekends. Danny couldn't find anyone else who wanted to do the protest, neither could I. He asked me if I knew anybody who would be willing to come out if they got paid."

Surprise rippled through Cady. "So Danny paid the other three protesters to be there?"

Betty Anne nodded then added somewhat defensively, "It happens in other protests, too. We'd have looked stupid if it was just the two of us. But five made it seem like a real protest."

Interest vibrated off of Kix and Cady knew he was thinking the same thing that she was—*follow the money*. There was no way that Danny's job at the animal shelter paid enough so that he could afford to "hire" protesters, and someone laying out their hard-earned cash wouldn't let the hired help sit around on long breaks or be as apathetic as Danny had been about the cause. "Did you and Danny pool your money to pay for the protesters?" Cady asked.

"No. Danny took care of it." Betty Anne looked around her apartment. "Paying for this place and my car insurance just about takes everything that I make."

Kix leaned forward, a portrait of compassion. "Betty Anne, do you think Danny was selling drugs to pay for the other three protesters?"

A sob wrenched its way out of her. "No!" She held up entwined fingers again. "We were like this. I'd know if he was doing something like that."

"What about the AFF? Do you think they were giving Danny money so he could hire the protestors?"

Even before the words had finished leaving Kix's mouth, Betty Anne was shaking her head vehemently.

"No. He was *not* in the AFF. We talked about it and he swore he wasn't a member."

Cady read between the lines and asked, "What made you think that he was a member?"

"I didn't think that." Betty Anne's face set in mulish resolve and Cady could see that they weren't going to get her to admit either what she knew or what she suspected about Danny's involvement in the AFF. It didn't matter though. If the AFF had paid Danny, Cady figured that they'd expect their money's worth, and they'd check to make sure they were getting it.

"Did you ever see Danny talking with anyone who worked at the track?" Kix asked, his hand brushing across Cady's knee as he silently requested the manila envelope containing the pictures of Angel Valdez talking with his agent and Angel receiving the box from Danny.

"No," Betty Anne said, her eyes drawn to the folder that was now in Kix's hand.

He pulled out the picture of Angel and Fats first. "What about either of these men?"

"No."

"When you were with Danny, did you usually go to his house, or did you usually come here?"

She licked her lips. "Usually here. But sometimes there."

Kix studied her intently for several long moments before saying. "Are you positive you haven't seen either man?"

"Positive."

His fingers slipped inside the manila envelope and even though Cady already knew what was inside, the tension he was creating was thick and uncomfortable and compelling.

A small thrill of pride went through her. He really was good at his job.

"Did you ever see Danny passing off index card sized boxes?"

The mulish look reappeared, but it was tinged with nervousness and anger. "He *wasn't* a drug pusher and if you think he was, then you can leave right now." She looked at Cady accusingly. "You said you wanted to help!"

Cady felt trapped, not sure whether she should jump in and play the part of "Danny's advocate" or remain quiet so that she didn't interfere with Kix's rhythm.

He sighed and slid the photo out just far enough for it to be obvious that it had been taken in a city. "Betty Anne, this photo might be alarming to you, so brace yourself," Kix said in a compassionate law officer voice.

"Right now the police looking into Danny's death don't have a copy because it seems to me that someone was trying to set your boyfriend up. Tomorrow the police are going to do an autopsy. If it turns out that Danny was murdered, then they're going to start looking around for reasons why and the chances are, they'll settle on him being killed because he was dealing drugs." Kix held his hand up to stop her protest. "I'm saying that's what the police investigating Danny's death are going to want to settle on. It's not necessarily the answer I'm happy with. That's why I need your cooperation to get to the bottom of this."

He pulled the photo out and set it on the coffee table. "Have you ever seen any of these little boxes in Danny's car or in his house?"

Betty Anne teared up and pressed a wadded tissue to her nose. She shook her head. "Never."

"Did you ever overhear any conversations about things going on at the track?"

The tears started to fall. "We didn't talk all that much. I mean, not about the track. Mainly we talked about other stuff, like why people wanted to wear real fur coats and why it was so hard to get anyone to care about how their food was raised."

Kix pulled a pen out of his shirt pocket and wrote B, BCC, AV on the manila envelope. "Do any of these initials mean anything to you? Most likely they're people."

Betty Anne's face furrowed in concentration and her lips moved as she silently read the initials. But once again she shook her head. "No."

"What about Danny's friends?" Kix prodded.

"The only people I met were either other protesters when I went with Danny or people at the animal shelter. Sometimes I stopped by there when he was working. And I went to the banquet they held at the beginning of the year. We didn't do much with other people—not like going to dinner or the movies or anything."

Kix picked up the photos and slipped them back into the envelope, then reached for one of the anti-horseracing pamphlets on the coffee table. He wrote down his cell phone number. "If you think of anything, you call me, okay?"

"Okay."

They left a few minutes later. Once they were in Kix's truck, Cady said, "I think she was telling the truth about everything except the AFF."

"That's the way I read it, too."

Kix took her hand and placed it on the hard muscle of his thigh before covering it with his. Cady looked at their joined hands. It was so corny, but him doing that made her heart jump and flutter and her stomach go all weird and silly. "I think we should tackle Angel Valdez," she said.

"All in good time, little darlin'. Today's a race day, so he might not be easy to get a hold of without an audience." Kix gave her hand a squeeze. "Here's what I'm thinking. Why don't you head back to the grandstand and see if you can hook up with Ernie the Weasel. Maybe you can get a fix on where Roberto Gonzalez and Tiny Johnson are hanging out these days and why Ernie pointed you in that direction to begin with. In the meantime, I'll pay a visit to a few other folks and see if I can whittle this puzzle down a little closer to its true shape."

He brought her hand to his mouth and pressed a kiss against her palm. "And later we can hook up at your place and swap stories."

Chapter Twelve

As sure as there were oil wells and beef cattle in Texas, it was going to be a long, lonely trip to the doghouse once his little darlin' found out about this. But damned if he was going to put her out on the firing line.

Valdez was the key right now, but he wasn't the man behind what was going on at the track. Kix was willing to bet every one of his trucks plus throw in his silver-plated Winchester rifle on it.

He was still working through the situation, and for the most part he always favored a money motive when it came to crime. Trouble was, right now he just hadn't figured out who stood to make the most money by running off Adrienne.

Valdez's involvement was a real puzzler. Adrienne had put him up on some of her horses and he'd finished in the winner's circle more often than not. A man didn't usually cut off his own income just to get even.

Sure, Terry whipped Valdez in a fistfight, but according to Adrienne, Terry's father didn't own a share in any of the drugged horses. They belonged to other family members. And why was Valdez getting the coke from a race protestor paid to be there?

It stunk. It had from the beginning but now it was getting worse. Someone was pulling some mighty tricky strings to cover their ass and hide their real motive.

Kix's gut got tight just thinking about Cady coming to the attention of whoever was behind this thing. He didn't want her ending up dead in some fabricated "accident". Because that's what he was dealing with here, someone who liked to stay hidden in the shadows and put distance and confusing circumstances between himself and the crime.

Well, no time like the present to try and scare up some answers. Kix pulled his truck over and parked in front of the address that Adrienne had given him.

* * * * *

Red, Jimmy and Ernie were in their usual spot. They hailed Cady like a long lost gambling buddy.

"My good lady," Ernie said. "This is a surprise and a pleasure. Unfortunately there's only one race left on the program."

Red rolled his eyes. "Good to see you. You feeling hot again?"

Cady laughed. "Give me a second to look at my program."

Jimmy dug into the bag on his lap and retrieved a bagel. He munched loudly as he looked over the entries for the final race.

"Don't you ever go and look at the horses in person?" Cady asked. There was an enclosure where anyone could watch as the horses were brought in and saddled before going out to the track for the warm up and post parade.

"Naw," Jimmy said around the bagel. "That just confuses the issue. He tapped on the *Daily Racing Form*. "Everything you need to know is right in here."

She looked at Red for confirmation. He nodded in a serious manner. "A horse can be pig-ugly and it doesn't matter. The numbers don't lie."

Cady grinned. She couldn't help yanking their chains a little bit. "If the numbers don't lie, how come people like yourselves, who know how to read them, don't walk away rich every time they come to the track?"

Ernie sighed dramatically. "Ah, my good lady, you have hit upon the very thing that drives professionals, such as we are, crazy. The vagrancies of fate…the will of the gods…the fickleness of Lady Luck…"

"Jesus, Ernie," Red interrupted. "The problem is that the numbers don't tell the whole story."

Jimmy nodded. "Sometimes a horse is having a bad day. Sometimes a jockey screws up."

"And sometimes shit just happens." Cady said.

Ernie sighed. "My good lady, that's it in a nut shell."

Red looked up from his program. "Maybe I'm going to start playing church bingo instead of the ponies."

"It'd be too tame for you," Cady said. "Unless you're on the lookout for a nice widow. Then church bingo could be a lot of fun."

"Count me out," Jimmy said as he finished off a king-sized candy bar. "My luck with women is worse than my luck with the ponies."

Cady grinned. "Well, your luck just changed. I'm still walking around with some of my winnings. How about if I treat you guys to dinner after the last race? Is there a place around here where track fans like to go?"

Jimmy levered himself out of his chair to go place his final bet of the night. "Sticklers has the best burgers and fries around."

* * * * *

There was flash of recognition and fear in the jockey's eyes when he realized too late that he should have checked before opening the door. Kix pushed into the apartment and closed the door behind him.

"You know who I am and what I'm after," Kix said, towering over the much smaller man.

"I don't know nothing."

"Wrong." Kix opened the manila envelope and pulled out the photo of the coke hand off.

"*Madre de Dios.*"

Satisfaction rippled through Kix. He could smell the fear rolling off Valdez. "You've got bigger problems than doping Adrienne's horses. Your buddy in the picture is dead," Kix said, watching Valdez's reaction carefully.

The jockey tore his eyes away from the photo and if Kix was reading him right, Valdez's fear had just ratcheted up to a whole new layer and not because he was guilty of killing Meyers. "The cops found him murdered," Kix bluffed. "Right now they don't have his appointment book or a copy of this, so they don't know about you meeting up with Meyers just about every Monday. Here's your chance to try and work a deal, with me as the go-between."

Sweat started to bead on Valdez's forehead. "What do you want?"

"I want to know who told you to drug Adrienne's horses and why."

Valdez's gaze dropped to the photo again and Kix practically choked on the smell of fear rushing off the jockey, but Valdez said, "No one told me to do it. I did it on my own."

Kix shook his head. "Try again. You don't have a beef with Adrienne."

The jockey's eyes darted around his apartment as though he was looking for help. Kix shook the photo and Valdez's attention instantly locked on the picture. "Come on, Valdez, why take the fall for someone else? You tell me who wanted Adrienne suspended and I'll do what I can to see that the DA cuts a deal with you."

Valdez began shaking his head no before Kix even finished. "No one told me. I did it on my own."

Kix ground his teeth. He was between a rock and a hard place. Valdez wasn't going to roll on whoever was calling the shots. He was too afraid. And Kix didn't have jurisdiction in the case — hell, the ME hadn't even signed off on cause of death yet for Meyers. The photo coupled with the appointment book was circumstantial evidence at best.

Kix pulled out his badge and a pen, then sweat Valdez some more — sweat him enough to get a signed confession on the back of the photograph.

It wouldn't stand up in a court of law, but it didn't need to, not if it caused whoever was jerking Valdez's strings to do something stupid, or made Valdez spook and come clean.

Still, Kix didn't like walking away from Valdez. It was a calculated risk, with a little insurance for Adrienne. If they had to, they could use the confession to clear Adrienne's name. But as far as Kix was concerned, he couldn't head back to Texas until he knew for certain that whoever had tried to ruin Addy wasn't going to get a second chance.

* * * * *

Sticklers was a block away from the track. The decorator theme was yard sale eclectic and though the sign on the door said maximum occupancy was sixty-five people, there probably weren't more than ten in the place, including the staff.

Jimmy led the way to a table at the back of the room. A waitress followed a few minutes later. Cady ordered an omelet with fruit on the side, and a chocolate milkshake to wash it down. The men with her shook their heads and told the waitress they'd take the usual.

"Eating like that's going to kill you," Jimmy said when the waitress disappeared. "The body needs a certain amount of grease to keep things moving along. It's lubrication."

Cady leaned forward, a serious expression on her face. "I probably shouldn't be telling you this," she whispered. "It's what gave me the winning edge the other day."

"What?" Jimmy asked, leaning in so close that his nose almost touched hers.

"Purifying the mind and body, that's the ticket. No junk food, no sodas, just clean living and clean eating. If you adopt that lifestyle, your mind becomes open to the cosmos and you can look at a race program and just 'know' who's going to win."

The expression on Jimmy's face as he contemplated giving up all of the things he held most dear was so comical that Red snorted and slapped his thigh. Ernie hooted and laughed until tears formed at the corners of his eyes.

Jimmy grunted in disgust and leaned back in his chair. "You had me going for a few seconds. The way my luck's been holding, I'd almost be willing to try a diet—but then what would I be left with?"

A short balding man brought the drinks over and set them on the table. Red turned to him. "How you doing, Russell? Looks like business is slow."

"So what's new? Place is dead night after night. Used to be it was flooded on race days. Had to hire extra waitresses during a meet. Made my best money then. But it hasn't been like that in a couple of years."

"Besides business being the pits," Ernie said, "what's the news with you?"

Russell paused and glanced around, then took a seat and leaned in. Voice low, he said, "I've been hoping you'd show up. You hearing any whispers from your friends about the track maybe closing down?"

Ernie glanced over and caught Cady's eye briefly before asking, "What are you hearing, Russell?"

"Only heard it once. Valdez and Gonzalez were in here drinking a couple of weeks ago. I was shorthanded that night, so I was waiting the table myself. They were both drunker than I'd ever seen either of them, and more talkative than usual. So I asked if either of them had any hot tips—hell, why not throw some money away on the horses before this place drains me completely dry?

"Gonzalez said, 'I got a hot tip for you, Russell. Say *adios* to racing. Pretty soon the only thing that's going to be here are apartment buildings and condos.

"That set Valdez off on a tirade. Far as I could tell every other word was a curse word." Russell shook his head sadly. "The Spanish was too fast for me to catch any of it. And when I asked Gonzalez what he meant about apartments and condos, he acted like it'd all been a joke.

"Afterward I started thinking about how dead the track is and how much rent I pay for this place, and how the land that the racetrack is sitting on has got to be worth a pile of money. Hell, it's about the only place around to build…" He shrugged again and looked at Ernie. "So you hear anything about the track closing?"

Before Ernie could answer, Red stabbed a french fry into a pool of catsup. "I can't see 'em closing the track down. Place is a landmark."

Russell shook his head. "Times have changed. Everywhere you look they're tearing places down and putting up townhouses and apartments in its place. I've gotta tell you, and I hate to say it, but the reason I'm so interested in the rumor is because I'd like it to be true. In the old days, the track was good for business. But now, I'm dying here. I've got a few regulars from the track that still come in. But that's it. A bunch of apartments and townhouses, they'd be good for business. Folks'd start seeing this place as the friendly neighborhood bar. Maybe I'd even get to hire more staff and go on vacation a couple times a year."

"I still can't see it," Jimmy said. "Beside being a landmark, you'd have to get the Johnsons to agree. That'd be one hell of a fight. Hell, they aren't even talking to each other half the time."

Russell's shoulders slumped. "Yeah, there is that."

The waitress came by with the bill. Cady pulled out the wad of cash and peeled off enough to cover it, plus a good tip and got a grateful smile.

As they walked back toward the racetrack parking lot, Cady moved in next to Ernie. "You never answered Russell's question about whether or not you'd heard anything about the racetrack closing down."

Ernie slid a smile Cady's way. "I've been hearing things, things that make me think Roberto is the man you want to talk to."

"The trouble is, Roberto Gonzalez is a hard man to find these days."

"For a visiting Texas sheriff, yes, but not for a photographer who just happens to be Bulldog Montgomery's granddaughter."

Chapter Thirteen

Kix was still thinking about the meeting with Valdez when he parked in front of Cady's house. Damn, if he didn't know better, he'd say that was guilt festering in his gut and not just indigestion from the burger loaded down with California beef. But hell, since when did a law officer share everything he knew with a civilian—even if that civilian was a mighty fine PI and a heck of a woman?

He stiffened his resolve. Start as you mean to go on. Hadn't that always been his motto when he was training a deputy or working a suspect?

He hadn't even told Adrienne about his little chat with Valdez when he stopped by her place and asked her to put the sealed envelope containing the confession in her office safe, and if anyone deserved to know, then it was Addy! But the way he saw it, there were too many things in play that he hadn't gotten a handle on yet.

The confession and the photo of Valdez and Meyers along with the police report about the coke, well all put together, they'd probably be enough to get Addy's license reinstated. But he needed a day to hunt down Tiny Johnson and maybe sweat some information out of him—'cause based on everything he'd been able to learn about the man, Tiny's brain wasn't much bigger than his name. And sure as the sky was always prettier over Texas, he didn't believe for a minute that Tiny could put a complicated plan in motion or come up with the money to fund it any more than he could turn out winning racehorses.

Sighing, Kix grabbed the bag in the passenger seat then climbed out of the truck. He was damned whatever he did. If he told Cady what he'd been up to, then he'd have to worry that she'd hare off and maybe get hurt. But if he didn't tell her right away, then he stood a good chance of spending a cold, lonely spell in the doghouse.

He squared his shoulders and headed for the front door. Well, granted, she wasn't like most women, but in his experience, they all came around with some good loving. And in the meantime, there was no defense like a good offense.

His cock jumped at the thought of exactly what he was planning. No time like the present to experiment, though damned if he wasn't going to pay the price when he got together with his brothers for some poker. He chuckled and shook his head. What was the world coming to when a man had to track down his younger brother and grill him about butt plugs? But hell, he'd walked into that little specialty shop and been confronted by more choices than a rancher at an auction.

Now, normally he prided himself on being willing to ask strangers some pretty tough questions, but he'd had to draw the line in that particular shop—not that the man running it wouldn't have been more than willing to help. Hell, there was no doubt in Kix's mind by the way the guy had fluttered his eyelashes and swished his hips that he'd had plenty of firsthand experience with things being shoved up his ass.

Kix had not wanted to go there! Not that he cared what a man did in his bedroom or who he did it with, as long as it wasn't breaking any laws. But he had not wanted to hear any personal comments on the virtue of one device over the other. So lacking time to hunt up another shop only to be confronted with the same overwhelming selection of sexual aides—he mentally sniggered at that—he'd called Walker.

Kix shook his head. Oh yeah, these cards would end up on the table. No way would his brother keep this to himself. And next poker game, Kix was sure to end up the sorry, sore butt of a lot of jokes.

* * * * *

Cady's heart jumped at the sight of Kix coming up her walkway. Damn, that loose-hipped cowboy walk and crooked smile warmed her from the inside out.

Ranger cocked his head and padded over to where she stood by the window. She gave his ears a quick rub before moving to the front door and opening it. The wicked gleam in Kix's eyes combined with the lethal smile had her clamping her legs together. "I did a little shopping, darlin'. Why don't we head on back to the bedroom?"

Her eyes dropped to the bag in his hand and her cheeks heated. Did he mean what she thought he meant?

Kix's husky laugh had her looking at his face. She shivered at what she read there. Part of him was teasing, seeing if she'd really go through with acting out his fantasy. The other part of him was hot and hungry and dead serious about his intentions.

She licked her lips nervously and he pulled her into a hug. "Trust me, darlin'."

"I do," she whispered back, allowing him to lead her to the bedroom door.

He paused and removed something from his pocket then tossed it to Ranger. "Here you go, partner." At Cady's quizzical expression he laughed. "Beef jerky." Then he ushered her into the bedroom and closed the door behind them.

Kix tossed the bag onto the bed and pulled Cady into his arms once again. "Anytime you want to say no, you say it," he whispered against her mouth before pressing his lips to hers, his tongue thrusting and stroking and twining with her tongue until Cady's cunt pulsed and her hips ground against the thick, heavy ridge of his erection.

The need for breath came second to the need to feel skin against skin. Almost desperately Cady's fingers fought with the buttons of his shirt. When his shirt parted, her hands traced the muscles of his chest, finally settling on the hard, tiny points of his nipples.

Kix groaned, his hands cupped her buttocks and pulled her pelvis more tightly against his. Damn, it was hard to think about anything else but climbing on top of her and getting his cock into her wet heat. "Cady darlin'," he whispered, coming up for breath and forcing his hands to get busy with her clothes.

Even the few seconds it took to get out of their clothing was too much time. Cady was shivering with need, awed by the hard power of his body, by the way his cock jerked under her hand, its head glistening with arousal. When she ran her thumb over the silken skin, Kix's sharp indrawn breath and clenched buttocks, his hoarse, "You're killing me, Cady darlin'," built her confidence in a way that nothing else would have. She wanted to please this man, to be his fantasy.

His cock still in her hand, Cady slowly eased onto the bed. Kix laughed and followed her down, latching onto her breast as soon as her back hit the dark green comforter. Cady arched into him and he responded to her silent demand, his licks turning to dominating sucks and possessive nips until Cady was desperate for him. "Please, Kix," she begged, her fingers spearing through his hair as her legs widened in a silent plea for him to enter her. She cried out when he lifted off of her, his hands going to her hips and flipping her onto her stomach.

"Not yet, darling. Now get this pretty little ass into the air."

Cady shivered when she felt his rough hands smooth over her buttocks. Nervous arousal flared through her as she slowly pulled her knees under her.

His cock jumped at the sight of her obeying his command, at the underlying trust that had her fighting her cautious nature and nervousness. He brushed his fingers over her ass cheek, trailing downward until he could rub between closed thighs. Damn. Everything about her was a distraction. She was so hot and wet, so swollen that his penis was practically howling with the need to tunnel into her sweet cunt.

He wrapped his free hand around his shaft, desperate to reduce the pulsing urgency that was like a second, louder heartbeat. "Spread your legs," he growled, clamping down hard on his penis the instant she complied and her plump, wet folds were exposed.

He groaned, unable to stop himself from leaning over, from running his tongue through her slit, from tasting her. "Damn, Cady, I can't get enough of you," he whispered, pulling back and forcing himself to reach for the bag containing the plug, glad now that he'd taken care of what preparation he could beforehand.

She tensed and he eased the fingers of one hand back into her pussy, gathering her arousal and then using it to ease into her back entrance. "Relax, darlin'," he whispered, removing his fingers and taking a second to open a small container and lubricate the plug before pressing it against the pucker of her anus. She shivered and he moved so that he could trail kisses from the base of her spine upward until his tongue and lips were tormenting her sensitive ears, and all the while he eased the plug deeper into her tight, unexplored back entrance. They were both shaking and covered with a sheen of sweat by the time the flared base of the plug was pressed against her buttocks.

Cady felt like crying...screaming...begging, but all she could manage was a whispered, "Please, Kix."

It was enough.

He covered her body with his and pressed the head of his cock to the opening of her slit. "Damn darlin', you're so tight," he groaned, working himself in and sending waves of sensation pulsing through Cady, the pain and pleasure melding so intensely that they nearly overwhelmed her.

Kix felt like a snorting, lust-crazed bull. He'd never fucked his cock into such a tiny place before, and it was just about to kill him with pleasure. He buried his face against her sweat-slick shoulder as he pushed the last inch of penis into her and fought the need to pound in and out of her furiously.

"Easy, darlin'," he whispered desperately against the smooth skin of her shoulder. Her whimpers and pleas were eroding his control just as surely as the tight fist of her channel was sweet agony.

His cock was pulsing and straining, his balls tight and burning with the need for release. But damn he didn't want to move, didn't want to rush this moment of pure bliss. He wanted to savor the feel of her hot muscles squeezing and rippling along his penis as her delicate feminine body shivered in submission underneath him.

Goddamn, he hadn't counted on liking this so much, on facing the fact that he might need it. He should have though, should have realized that everything about Cady was pure addiction.

She moved, pressing backward and sending a rush of lava-hot need along his shaft, shattering his control. He couldn't stop himself from answering her silent plea, from pumping in and out, slowly at first, and then faster, his pants and groans echoing her own as he pushed them higher and higher until they both yielded to the pleasure of a mind-numbing release.

Chapter Fourteen

Cady came out of the bathroom, fresh from a shower just as Kix was slipping his cell phone back into the holder on his belt, his tense expression telling her that the call hadn't been good news. "What happened?"

"They found coke in Terry's locker at the track."

She moved to stand in front of him, her mind already examining the different possibilities. "What does Terry say?"

"She swears that she's never touched the stuff and doesn't know how it got there."

"Do you believe her?"

"Yeah. I think she's rabid as a junkyard dog half the time, but she's not dumb enough to mess with cocaine and lose the chance to ride. Hell, that's about the only good thing I can say about her—she's got a dream and she's pursuing it, personality aside."

"Will the track officials run a blood test on her?"

"They sent her to a lab for a blood-draw. Terry's suspended as of this morning. She can't even set foot on the grounds."

"This looks bad for Adrienne." Cady shook her head. "Why now? Why not plant this stuff in Terry's locker the day that Adrienne's horses raced with the coke in their systems?"

Kix's face became harsher, but there was the brief glimmer of guilty knowledge in his eyes, and despite everything that had happened between them, Cady suddenly had a hollow feeling that once again he was keeping something important from her.

"I've got to head out," he said.

"You're going to Adrienne's house?"

There was the slightest flicker in his eyes before he nodded. It was so slight that if Cady hadn't learned from the best, from Bulldog, about how to spot subtle tells, she'd have missed it completely.

The warm glow at the center of her heart faded. It looked like trust only worked one way with him. "I'd like to go with you."

The silence stretched for a long tense moment before he said, "Why don't we meet up at Adrienne's in an hour. You've got to see to Ranger and I want to run by the track and talk to some folks about this first. Addy said that the track officials are authorized to search for illegal drugs, but unless someone is dangerous or causing trouble, they don't go looking for problems."

"You're going to try and find out who was behind the search?"

Kix nodded and moved to where she was still standing with only a towel wrapped around her. He slipped a finger between her breasts and used the towel to pull her closer then leaned down and gave her a soul-searing kiss. "Give me an hour, then meet me at Adrienne's place."

Cady got dressed, let Ranger out in the backyard before feeding him, then decided to take him for a walk before fixing her own breakfast. Her stomach felt queasy, like she'd just stepped off a roller coaster ride that had taken too many turns and too many steep drops. The sensation deepened, changing shapes, and shifting from Kix to the case when Cady finally got a chance to look at the newspaper and saw the small article at the bottom of the page.

Jockey Jumps From Golden Gate Bridge

The body of Angel Valdez, a popular jockey at Bay Downs and Golden Gate Fields, was retrieved by the Coast Guard early this morning. The Coast Guard was called to the area when fishermen found the body under the bridge. According to authorities, Valdez's car was found parked near the entrance to the bridge. No note was found, but a substantial amount of cocaine was in the car. Authorities suspect that Valdez was under the influence of drugs at the time of his death, but until the medical examiner completes an autopsy, this cannot be confirmed.

Cady's first instinct was to call Kix. She even went so far as to reach for the phone before remembering his hesitation, the small flicker in his eyes.

She gathered the newspaper and Ranger instead and left for Adrienne's house.

Kix was there, already in a heated argument with Terry McKay. They paused when Adrienne led Cady into the office.

"I guess you heard the news about Valdez," Cady said, taking a seat and putting the folded newspaper on her lap.

Adrienne's eyebrows drew together. "What news?"

The roller-coaster ride sensation returned with a rush and Cady knew that wherever Kix had gone, it hadn't been to the track. "They found Valdez in the bay. Right now the authorities are saying he may have been high on coke when he jumped off the bridge."

Cady offered the newspaper to Adrienne but Terry screamed incoherently and snatched it. Within seconds Terry's face was buried in her hands, her sobs filling the room.

Adrienne joined her cousin on the couch and slipped an arm around Terry's shoulders while Cady and Kix waited for the storm to pass.

Kix could see the writing on the wall as clearly as if it was painted there in blood. Trouble was coming. His little darlin' knew he hadn't been up-front with her.

Damn. He'd hightailed it over to Valdez's place when he should have headed for the track. If he'd done that then he would have known about the jockey's dive off the bridge.

His gut tightened and sickened. He'd played that one wrong, too. He'd figured that whoever was behind this thing would either back off or maybe do something stupid like come after him. He hadn't counted on the jockey ending up dead. And he wasn't ready to buy a suicidal dive off the Golden Gate Bridge, not on the heels of a protestor's death being set up to look like an overdose.

Damn. All he'd wanted to do was get this mess settled and keep Cady safe. Now he was going to have to come clean about the visit with Valdez. He couldn't afford to sit on the evidence, not with the police looking into Valdez's death, not when he was pretty sure that the ME was going to determine that the protestor's death was murder.

And as soon as he told Adrienne about Valdez's confession, she was going to insist on heading straight for the race officials so she could get her suspension lifted. Not that Kix blamed her for that, but... Hell, that wasn't even the worst of it. Cady was going to be mad. And hurt.

Kix rubbed his chest. Hurting Cady and seeing it in her eyes when she looked at him was going to feel like a knife slicing into his heart.

Terry's sobs petered out, replaced by gulps and the sound of air struggling through clogged nasal passages.

Kix took charge, though there was a hint of compassion in his gruff voice when he said, "Let's get this over with and put it behind us, Terry. Start talking about Valdez."

A couple more gulps and sobs followed the command, but then Terry nodded. "I was so stupid. I thought he loved me."

"You were dating him?" Adrienne looked like her head might start spinning. "I thought you hated him!"

Another gulp of air, now followed by hiccups. "I do hate him. Now." Terry paused long enough to draw in a steady breath of air. "I caught him in a stall fucking one of the exercise riders."

"Was that the day you got into a fistfight with him after a race?" Kix asked.

"Yeah."

"Did you know he used coke?"

Terry nodded. "We argued about it almost every time I went to his apartment. He started using it after he took that bad fall in January. Something happened, he lost his nerve. He said the coke helped him. He had family depending on him, he said. Most of what he made got sent back to Mexico."

Adrienne nodded slowly, a look of reluctant realization forming on her face. "I remember that spill." She took a deep breath. "When the horses tested positive for coke, did you suspect him?"

Terry wouldn't meet her cousin's eyes. "Just because I caught him fucking that slut, it didn't mean he'd wreck your career just to get at me. He rode for you sometimes. He always said you were a fair trainer. And he liked the horses."

"Answer the question," Kix growled. "Did you suspect him of doping the horses?"

Terry flashed him a hateful glance, her grief starting to meld into her normal personality. "Yeah. Are you satisfied? I suspected him, but he kept avoiding me. So I never got a chance to talk to him about it. You're the hotshot who is supposed to get Adrienne back on the track. So don't blame me if you didn't talk to Angel before now!" She leaped from her chair and ran from the room, slowing only long enough to slam the door behind her.

A muscle twitched in Kix's cheek. Adrienne ran a shaky hand along the edge of the sofa cushion and said, "What now?"

Kix sighed. It was just as well that Terry had stormed off. He'd just as soon not have her here to witness this. He shot a glance over at Cady and his chest went tight at the sight of her wary eyes and tense features. Turning back to Addy he said, "Go ahead and get one of those envelopes I gave you out of the safe. Get the one with the C in the corner."

Surprise and a touch of hope flared in Adrienne's eyes as she rose and moved to a floor-model safe behind her desk. Kix leaned forward, thinking to take Cady's hand in his and felt a stab of pain when she settled deeper in her chair, her body language warning him off.

Adrienne returned with the envelope. Kix took it from her and opened it, pulling a photocopy of the picture of Valdez and Danny out, along with a copy of the confession. "I'd hoped to hold off using this," Kix said, setting them on the coffee table, "but that might not be a good idea now that Valdez is dead." His eyes met Adrienne's. "The originals are in your safe. Don't touch them. Don't tell anyone that you've got them in your possession. The police are going to want to take a look at them, probably take them in as evidence, and it'd be better if they didn't have a whole mess of fingerprints on them."

Adrienne nodded and said, "This is probably enough to clear me. I want a copy."

Her voice held all the determination that Kix had expected. "Getting back on the track isn't the end of it, Addy. We still don't know who was behind getting you suspended in the first place."

"I know that. But for now it's enough if the race officials think it was just a grudge because of Terry. I *need* to get back on the track."

Cady stood abruptly. "And I need to head out and tie up some loose ends."

"I'll walk you out." Kix left his seat, moving to take her arm but she avoided his hand.

"That's not necessary. The race officials are going to want to talk to you about Valdez's confession."

"I'll walk you out," he said through clenched teeth.

Cady straightened her spine and turned without speaking, her entire focus on escaping without breaking down in front of him. When he grabbed her arm before she could get her truck door open, she tensed and said, "When did you talk to Valdez? Last night?" The answer was in his eyes. He'd met with Valdez before he'd gotten to her house last night and… Humiliation rushed through Cady at the memory of how vulnerable she'd been, of what she'd allowed him to do. Pain charged in after the humiliation. They'd gone from the door to the bedroom in record time, not allowing for the possibility to discuss the case. Sex as a distraction. She didn't have to examine last night any further to see that truth. She tried to pull away from his grip. "Don't bother answering, Kix. Now let me go."

"Not until you listen to me, Cady."

"Then talk."

One look at her face and he could tell she wasn't going to believe a word he said. Goddamn. He needed to try and talk some sense into her. He needed to make things right, but damned if he knew how.

"Darlin'…" he began, his heart jumping painfully at the way her body vibrated with hurt, at the way her eyes flashed with disbelief and anger and a hint of tears. "Cady dar—"

Cady jerked her arm out of his grasp, knowing that she could only handle so much before falling apart, and the sound of his calling her that… Cady's chest went so tight that for an instant she couldn't breathe.

She ducked her head in an attempt to hide the tears that had fought their way through her emotional barricade and started streaming down her face. "I need to leave, Kix.

Please don't embarrass us both by dragging this out. From now on, anything I find out, I'll pass on to Alex and he can pass it on to Adrienne. You can get it from her."

The sight of her tears froze him in place long enough for her to escape. And then he cursed himself for not grabbing her up and holding on to her until he could get her to understand that he loved her, that he was doing what came natural to him, he was only trying to make sure his woman stayed safe.

Chapter Fifteen

Cady's heartbeat had slowed to a dull ache by the time she'd driven out of Adrienne's neighborhood. Well, she'd known that Kix was going to be trouble with a capital H for heartbreak, but somehow…

No regrets. I'm not going to have any regrets. That's what I promised myself.

He'd made her feel things she'd never felt, he'd given her the confidence to do things she'd only fantasized about doing. She wasn't going to be sorry that she experienced any of it. She was just going to be more careful the next time.

She could do caution again. She and Erin had always been reserved when it came to dealings with the opposite sex. So it was nothing new. A sob caught in her throat and the tears fell.

Ranger stood up on the backseat and whined. Cady brushed the moisture off her cheeks. "I'm okay boy, from now on it'll just be you and me on the case, along with a little bit of help from Lyric and Erin."

Thanks to Bulldog, the Montgomerys and the Maguires had grown up learning how to play whatever cards were dealt to them and there was no shame in folding when a hand went bad. But that didn't mean you lost your courage and quit the game.

She dialed Erin, wanting to hear her sister's voice. "Are you out on a photo shoot?" she asked when Erin answered.

"No, I'm at Crime Tells." There was a pause. "Are you okay?"

A long shuddering sigh escaped. "I'll be okay."

"Kix?"

"Yes."

"You want to talk about it?"

"Not on the phone."

"What about if I meet you at the ranch and we go for a short ride?"

"I need to do some research on the Net."

"Lyric's here. Hold on."

A second later Lyric asked, "Did you and Kix have a fight about the appointment book?" Her voice conveyed just what she thought about that possibility.

"No." Then knowing that it was pointless to try and put off talking about what had happened, Cady said, "I thought we were working together, but we weren't, not really."

"He used you?"

Cady's stomach cramped. She refused to think that she'd been used. That would make the pain unbearable. "No. He got a confession out of Angel Valdez last night, but he didn't tell me about it until this morning at Adrienne's…when he had to."

"What was his excuse for holding out on you?" Lyric's anger flashed hot and volatile through the phone.

Cady hiccupped a sob. "I didn't stick around to ask him." *I didn't want to risk having him lie to me and make it worse.* Cady took a deep breath and tried to force the tightness out of her chest. If she could just focus on the case and get it behind her, then she could…move past this. Maybe afterward, when it wasn't so raw, she could take things apart and understand why he'd done what he'd done, but right now, she just wanted to escape from the hurt.

"It's not important, Lyric. I'll get over it. It just didn't work out, that's all…and besides, it's not like there was a future for us. He'll be heading back to Texas soon."

"Well, I think he's a—"

"Lyric," Cady interrupted, not wanting to hear Lyric get going on the subject of Kix.

"I was just going to say that he's a fool. It's not like you let very many guys close to you… He's a fool and an ass for hurting you, and I hope his dick—"

Cady's soggy laugh escaped and cut Lyric off. Cady took advantage of it and said, "There's a good chance that Adrienne will have her suspension lifted, but Alex hired us to find out who was behind it. Maybe it was just Valdez getting even with Adrienne's cousin, but I think it's more than that. There are some things I want to follow up on. Do you have time to do some research on the Web?"

"Sure. No problem. Besides, I want to see your dog. Why don't I dog-sit while you and Erin ride your horses?"

Cady's spirits lightened. News traveled fast in the Montgomery family. Erin must have seen Ranger and passed the information on to Lyric.

"I got him at the shelter. They were just getting ready to take him to the euthanasia room." Cady shuddered.

"God, Lyric, I don't see how you handle going to the shelter day after day."

"I do what I have to do. So do you have any background information on him?"

"Not much. Just that he's five years old and was already neutered."

"If you give me a copy of your adoption paperwork, I'll do a little investigating."

"That'd be great. I can swing by the house and get it. I should probably leave Danny's appointment book at the office, too, just in case Kieran needs it." Cady nibbled her bottom lip. "Did he confiscate your master keys?"

"It was a close call, but he got a little distracted meting out my punishment for…" Lyric snickered and Cady could just picture her sister rolling her eyes, "for being a bad influence on *you*, if you can believe that."

A fresh wave of pain rippled through Cady as she remembered Kix's teasing threat of a spanking and what it had led to. She held her breath in an effort to keep the tears at bay. Erin was right. From now on, no cops, no detectives, no bounty hunters, no one involved with law enforcement. In fact, maybe no one at all for a while. She'd just spend more time developing her photography business, and maybe she'd ask Cole if she could help him put on some of his poker clinics, or even go with Braden to some poker tournaments. She would stay so busy that she didn't even have time to think about K—about the opposite sex.

"You still there?" Lyric asked.

"Yeah, just thinking." Then to cover the nature of her thoughts, she added, "Just so you'll know, Danny might have been a member of the Animal Freedom Front. But I think he was probably in a cell that devoted itself to the anti-fur and anti-factory-farming cause, not animal research."

"Oh shit! Kieran is going to freak. I'll be under house arrest when he finds that out. Special Agent Lucero is still on the scene!"

Cady's smile wobbled into existence. It was hard not to feel a rush of warmth at the way Kieran and Lyric were so perfect for each other. Until he'd come along, Cady had spent a lot of time worrying about Lyric. Now she hardly worried at all.

Lyric didn't take nearly the number of risks she used to. Oh, her sister still talked tough, still had an uneasy relationship with rules—especially the ones that she didn't think should apply to her, but overall it seemed like Lyric's wild edge had blunted—at least outside of the bedroom, or the kitchen, or the hallway…or anywhere Kieran and she happened to be when they sparked off each other and just about set the place on fire.

"Then I guess the Crime Tells team had better wrap this up fast so you won't get locked up," Cady said, "and if it's any consolation, I don't think the AFF is behind it. So here's what I'm thinking. Kix told me that there were at least eleven other trainers who've been suspended for drugged horses since the beginning of the year, and I know there have been three fires at the track. What I'm wondering is whether or not there have been any other strange events. I'm also wondering if any rumors about the track being closed have hit the Web."

"Good angle. You're wondering if someone is creating a little mayhem so the place will shut down. I'm on it." There was a slight pause. "Oh, hey, Erin said she'll head out now and catch Joker and Ace while you swing by here."

"I'll be there in a few minutes."

* * * * *

No matter how hard he tried, Kix couldn't get Cady out of his mind. Damn, he felt worse than a dog whose nose had been shoved into its own mess before being kicked out into the cold.

His gut was roiling and his conscience was flaying him alive. Hell, all he'd wanted to do was make sure she stayed safe. But in the end, that'd turned around and bit him on the ass.

He'd screwed up. He was man enough to admit it. He was man enough to apologize if she'd give him half a chance.

But that was a mighty big if.

His heart felt like someone had it in a vise grip. His thoughts were a movie reel that was stuck in the same loop, a close-up of Cady's face with her trembling lips and pain-filled eyes, her body board-stiff as she hung on to her pride while her trust in him shattered like a fragile piece of crystal.

Kix rubbed a hand over his heart. This wasn't the kind of mess a man got out of with flowers or pretty words. This wasn't the kind of trouble that went away with some loving. The vice gripping Kix's heart tightened down a couple more notches as he got her voice mail again and hung up.

Hell, now he had no idea what she was doing or where she was. Now he had no way of keeping her safe.

He felt damned helpless and he didn't like it.

Kix gritted his teeth and forced his mind back to the case. It was time to wrestle this thing to the ground and tie it up like a cow for branding. The sooner he got that done, then the sooner he could turn his full attention to the most important thing in his life—his relationship with Cady. And come hell or high water, if he had to kidnap her and keep her prisoner in one of the Kicking A line shacks until she'd agreed to let him back into her life and her heart, then that's what he'd do!

* * * * *

Lyric's expression was fierce as she watched Cady's truck disappear from view. If she weren't married to a cop, she'd seriously consider finding Kix and doing some major bodily damage to him for hurting Cady.

Yeah, Cady and Erin both had the "stiff upper lip" thing down pat, but she had never been fooled by either of her sisters—not that they'd exactly been risk takers who let themselves get hurt very often, especially when it came to the opposite sex. Lyric shook her head. She loved Erin and Cady dearly, wouldn't trade either one of them for a pot of riches or a custom-built Harley, but sometimes it was hard to believe that they were raised in the same family.

Oh, she knew where they got their wariness from, that was easy to see. It came from watching the way every one of their male cousins left a trail of heartbreak in their wake. Seeing that kind of thing wasn't exactly the way to develop a lot of trust when it came to romantic relationships. But dammit, why'd this have to happen the first time Cady finally decided to go for the gusto!

Lyric clenched her hands. One minute alone with Kix, that should do the trick. A quick feint with her fists while her knee got him in a place that was guaranteed to make an impression. He'd think twice before hurting Cady again—if Cady would even let him close to her.

Lyric sighed...not if, but when. Cady was too softhearted to give Kix the cold shoulder and dick-twisting that he deserved. Knowing Cady, when Kix finally caught up with her, she'd listen to his explanation, tell him that she understood and she didn't hate him, then she'd wall up the pain and use it to keep the next man who came along at a safe, no-way-am-I-letting-you-close distance.

Damn, what really bit was that Kix and Cady had seemed so right together. Hell, Lyric would have bet the entire pot on it.

Lyric turned her attention to the gorgeous shepherd that had positioned itself near the front door as though he was waiting for Cady to get back. Well, at least Cady had Ranger now. Dogs were great to cry all over and confide in. No embarrassment, no worry that secrets would get blabbed. Yeah, a dog could be a real lifesaver. She punched in the number for her contact at the shelter. Now to find out a little bit more about Cady's new companion.

A few minutes later she had what she wanted—a name, Jackson Ford, and a phone number. She didn't waste any time calling.

Three rings and a man's voice answered. "Jackson."

"I'm calling about Ranger."

"Why are you calling about that goddamn dog?"

"A friend of mine saw him at the shelter and was thinking about adopting him."

"Goddamn dog is a lethal weapon. Fucking shelter shouldn't even have him up for adoption. I'd have taken him into the backyard and shot him myself if the neighbors wouldn't have called the cops. Fucking idiots, all of them. When I signed the papers the gal with the knockers said they'd put him to sleep."

"Why'd you want him put to sleep?"

"Goddamn dog went for me. Son of a bitch would have killed me if he'd had any fucking brains. Lucky for me I had a two-by-four handy. Stupid shit grabbed the board instead of my arm."

"Where did you get Ranger?"

"Fucking idiot son of mine brought him home with him. I told him not to bring the goddamn dog up here. I got a couple of Rotts already and it was a pain in the goddamn ass keeping the dogs separate. Last fucking thing I want is to get my ass hauled into the police station for disturbing the peace or dog fighting."

"So he's your son's dog?"

"Not anymore. Fucking idiot is in Elmwood. I told him the goddamn dog wouldn't be here when he got out. In for forgery and passing bad checks, fucking idiot. Got no brains or balls to get picked up doing pansy crimes like those."

"How long did your son have Ranger?"

"Goddamn idiot got him right after he got out of the joint the last time."

"When was that?"

Ford didn't make any effort to cover the receiver as he bellowed, "When'd Junior get out the last time?"

A woman's voice yelled, "January."

"Fucking idiot hasn't even been out a year."

"Any idea where your son got the dog?"

"Got him from some friends down in San Diego. Stupid shit, nobody ever gives you something for nothing. Dog's a goddamn lethal weapon."

"Do you know who the friends were?"

"No. I got my own problems. I don't need any more. He knows better than to bring his friends around here."

Jackson Ford hung up, but the conversation had only intensified Lyric's curiosity. Elmwood. She'd never visited a prison before... Then again, she'd better run it by Kieran first. Not that she needed his permission, but he was a cop, and she did care about his reputation.

* * * * *

Kix's heart rate jumped when the cell phone rang, but slowed when he saw it was Kieran. Damn, against all logic, he'd been hoping it was Cady.

"You're living dangerously," Kieran said as soon as Kix answered the phone. "And as a personal favor, I'd appreciate it if you'd start running if you see Lyric heading your way. I don't want my wife arrested for assault and battery."

Kix chuckled weakly. "News travels fast."

"And the family loyalty runs deep. I assume you held back telling Cady about the Valdez confession because you were trying to keep her safe?"

"Something like that."

"Not that I disagree with your thinking, but that kind of thing doesn't go over too well with the Montgomerys or the Maguires."

"Any idea what Cady's up to?"

Kieran snorted. "I'm not exactly on the short list of people the Montgomery sisters trust with information right now. For some reason, even my own wife seems to think that lawmen will stick together. She wouldn't tell me anything and when I tried to persuade her, that dog of Cady's came at me like a police dog. The sight of all those teeth just about killed a great hard-on."

"I'll keep that in mind," Kix said, glad for the warning and the knowledge that at least Cady had some protection. "Anything from the ME?"

"Yeah. The Meyers case is going over to homicide. The ME found tranquilizers in him. Thinks he was out cold when someone shot the coke in him."

"What about his phone records?"

"Nothing. Looks like he used the phone to talk to his girlfriend and to call his workplace. That fits if he's a member of the AFF. Probably used payphones and disposable cells for any of his important calls."

"Damn. You have any contacts in the San Francisco PD?"

"This is off the record, same way that I got it. The only person Valdez called last night was Luke Johnson. Sounds like it happened late, after your visit. You might want to give Detective Giancotti a call. Word is that he's going to do the preliminary investigation on Valdez's death. Right now it could go either way—suicide or murder. I assume the confession you got is out in the open?"

"Yeah, I couldn't hold Adrienne off. She wants her suspension lifted. She's probably meeting with the race officials right now."

"Too bad she wouldn't sit on it for another twenty-four hours. Maybe you could have used it to flush out whoever killed Meyers and probably killed Valdez." Kix sighed. "I've got to head to the captain's office. Another heads up, the Meyers case is going to Butler in homicide, the tie-in with the track is more complex than he's going to like. He's not going to want to look past the coke and the possibility that it was a rival drug dealer."

"That might work to my advantage right now. I need to get this thing wrapped up."

"The quicker, the better—and much appreciated on this end. A Montgomery wife on the warpath is not a pretty situation to face at the end of the day."

Chapter Sixteen

There was something about being with horses that brought Cady's world back into balance. Between riding Joker and crying and talking, she felt calmer and more centered than when she'd gotten to the ranch. "This was a good idea, thanks for putting up with me."

Erin laughed softly. "All for one and one for all. So what's your next move?"

"I keep thinking about what Russell said last night. If you lump Adrienne's problem together with three fires, some of the other suspensions, and the protesters out front, then the motive almost jumps out and hits you in the face."

"Someone wants to shut down the track."

Cady untied Joker's lead rope from the hitching post. "If it were more organized, then I'd say the AFF was behind this. But if they were paying protestors, then they'd want their money's worth. Even then, I'm not sure if they would risk hurting the horses."

"So you're thinking that someone in construction or real estate development is behind this, someone who wants to put condos or apartments where the track sits?"

"Maybe. But I don't know for sure. Do you remember that portrait I did of the African Gray parrot standing on his owner's shoulder with the *Wall Street Journal* as a backdrop?"

Erin laughed as they headed toward the gate leading to the pasture. "That was a great shot. Wasn't that bird's name Wall E. Street?"

Cady grinned. "Yeah, Wally to his friends and family. His owner is an investment guy. I thought I'd give him a call and ask him to look into the Bay Downs stock. I think I need to know what it would take for someone to get their hands on the land that the track is on."

Erin whistled softly. "Great idea. You might also find out that someone's been buying up the stock in order to force the issue."

They stopped long enough to open the pasture gate and lead their horses through before releasing them and watching as Ace and Joker galloped off to rejoin their herd. Cady smiled, actually feeling lighthearted. Yeah, there was just something about horses…

Turning back toward the parking lot, Erin sighed. "Well, I'm off to a photo shoot. Then Bulldog has invited me over for dinner."

Cady's eyebrows shot up. Not that she and her sisters weren't frequently invited to their grandparents' house, but usually it was Grandma Montgomery who did the inviting.

"What's up?"

Erin shifted uncomfortably. "I turned down a case today."

Cady was so shocked that her feet stopped moving abruptly and she almost pitched forward. "Bulldog asked you to take a case and you turned it down?"

"Yes."

Cady grabbed Erin's upper arm. "Okay, you listened to me blubber and cry about Kix, now it's my turn to listen to you. What gives?"

"Dasan Nahtailsh."

"The bounty hunter?"

Erin nodded. "He met with Bulldog this morning. He wants Crime Tells to investigate cheating at an Indian casino."

Cady frowned. Now Erin was making no sense at all. "You've worked a casino case before."

"Not like this. Dasan told Bulldog that the best way to go in was undercover, posing as his wife."

"Well, that knocks out Braden, Shane, and Cole. And I can't see Kieran agreeing to let Lyric pretend to be someone's wife—even if he and Dasan know each other. So that leaves you and me, and I'm still not sure why you said no."

Erin grimaced. "I'm attracted to him."

"You'd have to be dead or *extremely* gay not to be attracted him, Erin. The guy is a walking fantasy. At Lyric's wedding reception Grandma Maguire practically had to beat the women off of Dasan with her cane in order to get close enough to talk to him."

When Erin remained quiet, Cady studied her sister more intently and felt the first stirrings of amazed disbelief. "You're worried that you're going to sleep with him." Not that Cady couldn't understand the temptation, but Dasan was a bounty hunter and Erin had always been adamant that she would never get involved with any man whose job put him in danger. Though truthfully, Erin hardly ever got involved with anyone.

Guys had been hitting on Erin since before she'd even had breasts. But instead of making Erin vain, it had made her more conservative. And though Erin would never admit it out loud, Cady had always thought that her sister secretly wanted a dominant man who'd take charge so that she wouldn't have to stay so controlled.

Dasan could be that man.

Not that Cady had spent a lot of time around him. But he made her think of historical romance novels where Native American braves took their captive women out into the wilderness and thoroughly mastered them.

Shivering, Cady forced her mind back to the conversation. "You're worried that you're going to sleep with him?" she repeated.

Erin nodded slightly and rubbed her palms against her jeans in a nervous gesture. "You know he's a shaman, don't you?"

"Yes."

"Ever since that day Lyric got shot, I've been dreaming about him." She licked her lips. "Sometimes the dreams are…um…sexual, but not always." She shrugged. "I can't explain it, but they don't feel like ordinary dreams. They don't feel like they're just *my* dreams."

"Have you talked to Grandma Maguire about them? Maybe you're…"

Erin shook her head vigorously. "It's not the Maguire sixth sense. Look at Lyric and Braden. They've both had some of it since they were kids. This is different…like it's coming from outside of me, not inside."

Cady hesitated before plowing in. "Are you saying that you think Dasan is responsible for the dreams…that it's some kind of shaman magic?"

Erin shrugged and rubbed her arms. "I sound crazy, don't I? Too much work, not enough sex, that's what Braden, or Shane, or Cole would say. Hell, Lyric would probably say it too."

Cady chewed on her bottom lip. She'd never seen Erin like this. "I think Lyric would say that you should go for the gusto. Maybe you should…"

Erin interrupted with a shake of her head. "No. Not with Dasan."

* * * * *

Nathaniel Bradshaw's house was designed to entertain clients. It was plush, spotless, tasteful, and like Adrienne McKay's house, it could have been featured in *Architectural Digest*.

Trophy wife number four showed Cady into Nate's study where Wally the African Grey parrot was sitting on a play-tree and vigorously attacking a human-shaped toy while his investment guru owner hovered over a small table, glasses perched precariously on his nose as he studied the papers in front of him.

Nate looked up when Cady walked in. "I've been studying the numbers. Nothing spectacular here. Any particular reason you like this stock? There are a couple of other stocks out there right now that I'm very hot on."

Cady shook her head. "This has to do with a case that I'm working on. It's not exactly confidential, but it's sensitive."

Nate straightened and there was a speculative gleam in his eye. "Discretion and I are well acquainted. Does this have anything to do with the jockey they found in the bay?"

"Maybe."

"So what are you after?"

"I'm looking for a money motive to explain some of the things happening at the track. Specifically, I'm trying to sort out a rumor that Bay Downs might close so that the land can be used for condos and apartments. But I'm open to suggestions. You're the expert on this kind of thing. So if something jumps out at you…"

Nate had already started shuffling through the papers on his desk, the fingers of one hand dancing across the keys of a fancy little calculator. There was a muted exclamation and then he moved to the computer and worked there. The next time he looked up, his eyes were shiny with excitement.

"If the rumor is true, this stock is undervalued by a substantial amount. It could be worth almost four times its current trading price."

"How can you tell?"

He tapped one of the papers on his desk. "The primary asset of Bay Downs per the financials is the grandstand area, in other words, the building. The land is carried at cost. But the cost doesn't reflect fair market value. That land would be worth a fortune to a developer, especially someone who wanted to put residential property on it."

Cady tried to translate what he was saying into something that fit with the case. If she was hearing Nate correctly, then the stock of Bay Downs was a great candidate for someone to make a killing on—but only if the track was going to shut down.

Her thoughts stilled. Adrienne said she'd made five million last year between race winnings and betting on her own horses. And then there was the well-known fact that Adrienne came from money. Between her and her family, they could probably buy enough stock to prevent the closing of the track and maybe even run up the cost of the stock so it wasn't undervalued.

That would be plenty of motive for drugging Adrienne's horses and getting her license suspended...but was it enough motive for killing Meyers and Valdez or setting fires to three of the barns and ruining lesser known trainers?

Cady sighed, frustrated. If she could just talk to Roberto Gonzalez... Maybe he had the last piece of the puzzle, the piece that brought it all into focus. Ernie had said that Gonzalez was willing to talk to her...well, she needed him to talk *now*.

"Anything else jump out at you?" she asked Nate.

"There's been an increase in the number of shares changing hands since last year. Not enough to turn it into this week's hot tip in a brokerage house, but definitely enough to make me interested now that you've pointed it out."

Cady thanked Nate and headed to the track to dig around for some more answers, and to make herself accessible if Gonzalez was ready to talk.

Chapter Seventeen

The stench of failure and alcohol hit Cady as soon as she walked into the small dark space that served as Jamie Johnson's office. The trainer grunted and said, "Let me guess, you're the detective I've been hearing about. Would have figured you'd be off celebrating now that Adrienne McKay has her license back." He opened a drawer and pulled out a clouded glass and set it next to the one on his desk. "Drink?"

Cady shook her head, a small tremor of concern sliding along her spine. She hadn't anticipated…this. She's assumed that Adrienne would get her suspension lifted and that there would be rumors. But she'd expected Kix to star in them, not her.

"Okay if I sit?" Cady asked, moving to a dust-covered chair.

Jamie waved a hand. "Sure, sure." He took a swallow of the amber-colored drink in his glass.

When he didn't say anything else, Cady waded in. "There's a rumor that Bay Downs is going to close. Have you heard anything about it?"

Jamie snorted. "You mean the rumor about Bay Downs moving to Sonoma, about the fancy showpiece barns, and how it's going to save horseracing in Northern California?"

Cady's pulse skipped through her veins. She'd been testing the waters only to be pulled under. She bluffed her way through her ignorance. "You don't believe it?"

Jamie opened his arms wide. "I'm still in this same stink-hole, waiting for a lucky break. Somehow I don't see that big shot beating a path to my office and sharing his vision with me." He polished off his drink then reached into the desk drawer and pulled out a half-empty bottle of Jack Daniels, splashing some of it into his drink.

"By big shot, do you mean your brother Luke?"

Jamie's face twisted with distaste. "You want to keep talking to me, don't mention my brother's name."

"So whose vision is it to move the track to Sonoma, then?"

"Mr. Big Shot Barwig. The guy who owns Expansion and a couple of other nice horses. A little taste of the winner's circle and he thinks he's got all the answers."

Cady almost plowed into Luke Johnson and another man as she left the barn housing Jamie's office. "Sorry," she said, recognizing Luke from the research she'd done on the Johnson family. The man with him also looked familiar. "You're Luke Johnson, right?" She saw recognition flash in Luke's eyes but he nodded and said, "And you are?"

Her first instinct had been to ask him about the rumor, but his pretending that he didn't know who she was sent a whisper of caution through her. "Cady Montgomery."

"Ah, Bulldog Montgomery's granddaughter." His eyebrows drew together. "What brings you here? I thought I heard that Adrienne's suspension was revoked."

"I heard that, too," Cady said, dodging the question and refraining from confirming that she'd been investigating on Adrienne's behalf. She checked her watch and lied, saying, "I've got to head to a photo shoot. It was nice to meet you."

She'd planned to stay on the backstretch a little longer, walking around and making herself accessible in the hope that Roberto Gonzalez would come forward. After the encounter with Luke Johnson, she gave up the idea in favor of getting back to Crime Tells and doing an Internet search on Barwig, the owner of Expansion.

But when she got to her truck, there was a torn and folded piece of paper underneath her wiper bade. Roberto Gonzalez was finally ready to talk. He was waiting for her at Sticklers.

She got in the truck and drove the short distance to the diner, her heart aching as she retrieved her phone messages and heard Kix's voice. She'd see this case through to the end, but she wouldn't lie to herself. She wished that Kix was here with her—not for protection or for his expertise, but because being with him, sharing with him, made the colors in her life more brilliant.

Cady took a shuddering breath and pushed thoughts of Kix aside as she deleted his messages. Sharing had to work both ways, just as trust had to go both ways.

She got out of the truck and went into Sticklers. Russell wasn't there, but the waitress who'd been working the night Cady treated Red, Ernie, and Jimmy to dinner was. She smiled at Cady. "Take your choice of a place to sit. Besides the guy in the back booth, you're the only other customer."

"I'm supposed to meet someone." Cady looked toward the back booth and the Hispanic man sitting there. "Do you know who he is?"

The waitress's eyebrows rose in surprise. "Sure, that's Roberto. He trains over at the track."

Cady nodded in relief. "Thanks."

Roberto stood and offered Cady his hand when she got to the booth, and since he was eating, Cady took the time to order, then let silence hover over the table after the waitress moved away. There were a hundred questions that Cady wanted to ask and she knew it was a gamble not to plunge right in and try to get some answers before he changed his mind about talking to her, but her instincts told her to let Roberto start the conversation, to let him proceed at his own pace, in his own way. He didn't start until the waitress had returned with Cady's food.

"Angel didn't kill himself," Roberto said, his voice unaccented despite his Hispanic features. "He was Catholic and he had family that depended on him in Mexico."

"Then who do you think killed him?"

Roberto looked around the diner even though no one had entered since Cady's arrival. "Luke."

A shiver of uneasiness danced along Cady's spine as she remembered running into Luke Johnson and his casual, unspoken question about why she was on the backside of the track. "Why Luke?"

"He told Angel to drug Adrienne's horses."

Excitement shot through Cady. "Angel told you that?"

"Yes."

"You were friends?"

A struggle with grief took place on Roberto's face. A long moment passed before he said, "Yes."

When he didn't say anything else, Cady asked, "Did you know that Angel used coke?"

Another nod. "He had a fall and lost his nerve."

"Did you know he bought it from one of the protestors?"

"No. I never asked him where he got it."

"Why did you leave a note on my truck?"

"You know I work for Tiny?"

"Yes. Is he part of what's going on at the track?"

"Not part of it, but he knows something." Roberto settled more heavily into the vinyl bench seat and Cady got the impression that whatever war he'd been waging on the inside was finally over. "I don't have a green card," he said and she made the leap with him.

"So you can't go to the police about Valdez or anything else because you're afraid that you'll be deported."

"Yes."

"I can't promise anything except that I'll try to keep your name out of it and I'll ask Bulldog if he knows anyone who can help you with immigration."

Roberto hesitated for a second, then said, "Mostly Tiny has lousy horses and lousy owners. Last year he was scrambling for money. The hay man wanted cash on delivery, the farriers wouldn't shoe the horses unless they got paid up front, and a couple of times I bought food for the grooms because Tiny didn't have enough to pay them. But a couple of months into the first meet of the year, suddenly he has a lot of money. He told everyone that he won it in Vegas and that it was just the beginning of a lucky streak." Roberto shrugged. "I didn't care where it came from as long as I could keep training horses. But one night I stopped by the barn to check on a horse. Tiny was in his office with a stack of money. He's not a drinker like Jamie is, but that night he was drunk and talkative, laughing about how stupid Luke was, how only an idiot documented illegal activities in a business plan."

"So you think Tiny was blackmailing Luke."

Roberto nodded and sent Cady an anguished, half-pleading look. "I didn't understand what Tiny meant about the illegal activities. I closed my eyes and didn't think about it. It was such a relief not to have to worry about money. All I wanted was to get enough experience so that I could eventually train on my own. I didn't understand what was happening until Angel broke down and told me about drugging Adrienne's horses and a couple of other ones besides them. Luke knew about the coke, and he knew that Angel needed money for his family in Mexico." Roberto took a deep breath. "He also knew that Angel's papers were fake, that he was using his cousin's social security number so he could stay in the US and ride. Angel didn't have any choice but to do what Luke said."

"Do you know where Tiny is?"

Roberto hesitated for only a minute before writing the address down on a paper napkin. "He's staying at his girlfriend's place. She looks after the horses on lay-up there."

* * * * *

Frustration seethed along every one of Kix's nerve endings. He felt like he was standing in front of a wall and banging his head against it. The cops working both the Meyers' case and the jockey's suicide had pretty much said the same thing, "Thanks for the information. We'll take it from here," with a subtext of, *We don't need some out-of-jurisdiction cowboy to show us how it's done in the big city.*

And on top of that, Cady hadn't returned any of his calls. Damn, he couldn't stand this. He picked up the cell phone and called her again, only to get her voice mail. "We need to talk darlin', please call me."

Chapter Eighteen

Cady swung by Crime Tells to pick up Ranger, her heart filling with warmth at finding him waiting next to the door for her, devotion shining in his eyes and the slight wag of his tail acknowledging that he was happy to see her. "Other than doing a great imitation of a police dog when Kieran showed up, Ranger's pretty much spent all his time waiting next to the door for you to come back," Lyric said as Cady smoothed her fingers over the shepherd's ears.

"What do you mean by 'doing a great imitation of a police dog'?"

Lyric laughed. "Well, Kieran showed up for the appointment book. Being male and a cop, he made the mistake of trying to defend a certain sheriff from Texas. Things got a little, uh…heated…and Kieran ended up seeing Ranger's teeth."

Alarm radiated through Cady even though Lyric didn't seem upset. "Ranger attacked Kieran?"

"No." Lyric's attention shifted to the dog. "No. He acted like a police dog would act. Lunging and barking and holding Kieran at bay. I tried some German commands and Ranger responded. I think he's had some protection dog training. If you're up for it, maybe we can take him over to Protection Plus Canines and have Deuce McConachie put him through his paces."

"Sure, that'd be okay."

"Just brace yourself, Deuce is the stuff of fantasies." Lyric's eyebrows went up and down. "One look at him and you might decide to sign up for Schutzund classes with Ranger."

Cady's heart took a dive and even though she knew Lyric was just teasing, she said, "I think I'm going to take a break from men for awhile."

Lyric shook her head, but thankfully refrained from saying anything. "Any new leads in the case?"

Cady nodded and told her about the visit with Nate, and what she'd learned from talking with Jamie Johnson and Roberto Gonzalez.

Lyric frowned. "Barwig. That name sounds familiar. Hold on a second." She opened the folder containing Ranger's adoption papers along with a mass of other papers that Cady hadn't taken the time to read yet. A moment later, Lyric pulled out something that looked like a newsletter. "Here it is. There's a blurb about the donor/volunteer/staff recognition banquet that the shelter holds every year. One of the people honored was Helen Barwig. According to this, she was instrumental in raising the funds for building a 'get acquainted' area so people could visit with potential pets before adopting them."

Cady's heart pounded in her ears. There was a notation in Danny's appointment book about attending the banquet. She moved over to the desk. "Does it mention her husband?"

"Yeah, his name is Andrew." Lyric turned to the computer and entered the name. Within seconds the connection to Danny was obvious.

"Andrew Barwig, owner of Barwig Construction Company," Cady said. "BCC."

Lyric was already reaching for the case folder. A moment later they were looking at the copied page from Danny's appointment book. Two days after Danny had attended the banquet he'd met with BCC in San Francisco at 10 p.m.

Without being told, Lyric returned to the keyboard and dug a little deeper. "Barwig is based in San Francisco."

A couple of keystrokes more and Lyric pulled up a picture of Barwig standing in the winner's circle at Bay Downs with Luke Johnson at his side. Cady's skin crawled as she recognized the man she'd seen with Luke Johnson as she'd walked out of Jamie Johnson's barn.

"Odds are, Barwig is the "B" that shows up at the beginning of each month in Danny's appointment book," Lyric said, drawing Cady's attention away from the computer monitor and back to the photocopied pages of Danny's appointment book.

Cady sat down on the edge of the desk. "It's also possible that he's the one Tiny Johnson has been blackmailing and not Luke."

"My money would be on him as the brains behind the operation, and he'll be the biggest winner at the end of the day." Lyric grinned. "At the risk of getting a lecture and one of your severe frowns, a certain Texas sheriff is going to be sorry he decided to play lone ranger when you wrap this case up with a bow and shove it in his face—hopefully breaking his nose in the process."

"Lyric…"

"Okay, okay, I'm sorry. Well, not really, I'm just pissed at him for hurting you and if you'd just say the word…" Lyric's voice dropped into a gangster impersonation, "I got friends who could pay him a visit and show him the error of his ways...slowly and painfully."

Torn between crying and laughing, sadness over Kix and profound joy at having such great sisters, Cady leaned over and gave Lyric a hug. "Enough already. Let's just get this thing solved."

Lyric hugged her back. "You bet."

Cady pulled away and asked, "Did Kieran tell you what the ME found when the autopsy was done on Danny?"

"Murdered. They found tranquilizers in his system. He was probably out cold when someone shot the coke in him."

"What about Valdez?"

"Still up in the air. Kieran called someone he knows in the SFPD and gave them a heads up on how the case could connect to Danny's murder." Lyric shrugged. "No telling how the SF police department is going to play it. It's not like they don't have plenty of people try and go off the bridge—we just don't hear about them. If Valdez hadn't been a 'somebody' because he rides at Golden Gate Fields, we probably wouldn't have known about his death so quickly. For the last couple of years the media has really towed the line about not attracting copycats by giving jumpers publicity."

Lyric's comment blasted through Cady like a bolt of lightning. "Remember the photo club meeting that Erin and I dragged you to?"

"You mean the one where I had to tell the two of you a million times that your talk on 'Taking Award-Winning

Pet Portraits' was better than anything besides the invention of the Harley? That club meeting?"

Cady laughed, still feeling embarrassed about how stressed she'd been about talking in front of a huge group of people. "Yeah that one. Remember *The Ghoul*?"

"Oh yeah, I remember him. He had a permit to set up a camera and film the bridge 24/7 for a year. Man, he gave me the creeps talking about putting together a coffee table book on the Golden Gate Bridge—complete with jumpers. His sick little face lit up about already having pictures of three of them committing suicide." Lyric's eyes widened. "Shit, Cady, he might have caught Valdez going over."

"Can you track him down? I want to see if I can corner Tiny Johnson."

Lyric stood up and moved toward the filing cabinets. "I'm on it. Erin probably has a copy of the meeting program along with some contact numbers."

Cady picked up Ranger's leash and snapped it onto his collar. "Call me if you find anything."

* * * * *

Kix eased the white car away from the curb, careful to stay back far enough so that Cady wouldn't notice him. Damned if he wasn't a sorry sight. His brothers would sure howl if they could see him now, reduced to renting a nondescript car and skulking around after his woman until he got her alone and had a chance to talk to her.

It was not one of his finest moments.

Then again, if he couldn't talk her into forgiving him, his future was going to be made up of a whole string of bleak minutes.

* * * * *

Yummy, Lyric thought as she watched Dante Giancotti, the San Francisco detective assigned to look into Valdez's death, climb out of his unmarked police car. *Who'd have guessed that so many bad boys ended up cops?*

"Baby, if you don't stop staring at him, your ass is going to hurt for a week when I get done with you," Kieran growled, not liking the way his hot little wife was giving the other cop the once-over.

He moved into her so that her back was pressed to his front in a territorial display that screamed *mine*. The little hellion had the nerve to laugh and rub against his cock, sending a rolling wave of lust through him. When he got her home…

Lyric grinned. As excited as she was about making contact with *The Ghoul* and setting this meet up so they could go over his film of the bridge, a few minutes with Kieran and she was hot to get it over with so they could go home. Oh yeah, he was already worked up, already walking around with an erection that made her mouth water and her cunt slick. Lyric decided to torment him a little more just for good measure. She sent him a saucy, challenging look. "I'm married, Kieran, not blind, but I bet your sister would like him."

Every muscle in Kieran's body went taut. Son of a bitch, he hadn't seen that one coming. His gut was already churning at the thought of his baby sister interviewing with Bulldog. Goddamn. He didn't want her around Lyric's cousins, especially Braden, and he sure as hell didn't want Calista hooking up with Giancotti. Even if only one of the rumors about the other cop was true, it was one too many.

The cop in question was moving in too fast for Kieran to respond to Lyric's comment, and from the smirk on Giancotti's face, he was getting a kick out of something. Kieran tightened his hold on Lyric, feeling like a dog guarding its bone, but shit, he'd given up fighting the effect she had on him. "Let's get this over with," he growled.

Chapter Nineteen

Cady felt the first stirrings of uneasiness when she turned onto a dirt road and saw a barn in the distance, an ancient house trailer and a couple of cars sitting near it. When Roberto had said Tiny's girlfriend looked after horses that were being laid-up until their injuries were healed and they were ready to go back into training, Cady had envisioned a nice facility, not a run-down place in a remote area.

She reached over and rubbed Ranger's ears. "You're going to get out at this stop," she told him, his presence making her feel safer. As if sensing her worry, the shepherd was staring out the window, his eyes alert, his body tense and ready for action.

There was no way of sneaking up on Tiny, not with open fields and the trail of dust Cady's pickup was leaving behind on the dirt road. She half-expected someone to come out of the trailer or the barn, especially since there were two cars. When no one did, she thought about turning around, but there was no reason to think this was a setup, or that she was in danger. She opened her door and climbed out of the truck, tugging slightly on the leash so that Ranger jumped out.

* * * * *

Amusement rippled through Detective Dante Giancotti as he took in the way Kieran Burke was hovering and growling over his wife. Not that she wasn't a fine piece of ass, she was—and then some. But this was business and Dante never mixed business with pleasure. He also never got involved with married women. Why make things complicated?

He liked his women easy and he liked to share them with his brother.

End of story.

He sure as hell never felt the way Kieran obviously did about his wife.

"Ready?" he asked and they moved into the apartment building with Lyric leading the way. Three flights of stairs and a geek with slicked-back hair opened an apartment door, his face going from anticipation to dread when he saw that Lyric wasn't alone. They stepped into a hole of a room that had been arranged with seduction in mind.

Candles and chilled wine?

Dante grunted. Shit. Condoms and ice-cold beer had always worked for him. He leaned over and flipped on the light switch while keeping an eye on Kieran. He had to hand it to vice cop, Kieran was keeping his cool. The geek, on the other hand, was sweating.

"These guys are cops," Lyric said and Dante thought the geek was going to wet his pants. Out of habit his eyes roamed the apartment and he almost cracked a smile. Not that they were going to need it with this guy, but their leverage was sitting on the kitchen windowsill. *Cannabis Sativia*. Nothing like a pot plant in plain view to make for a cooperative visit.

The geek licked his lips and waved toward the computer. "The camera caught it last night. The murder. That's what you were after, right? The murderer must have known the cameras on the bridge wouldn't be able to see him in the fog. My camera wouldn't have either if the fog had layered up like it sometimes does." He licked his lips again. "After you're done with it, do you think I can use it in my—" Dante's glare cut him off.

They moved over to stand in front of the desk. The geek hit a key and the digital movie rolled forward, showing Luke Johnson guiding a barely functioning Valdez to the railing of the bridge and pushing him over, sending him to his death.

* * * * *

Kix's heart went into overdrive when Cady left the main road. He didn't like the looks of this and he didn't like the fact that she was going in alone.

He hit the gas and sent the rental car charging down the dirt road just as she climbed out of her truck. When she stopped and turned in his direction, relief rushed through him with the force of a one-ton bull. "Stay put, darlin'."

But it seemed like the words hadn't even left his mouth when something startled her. She spun toward the barn and Ranger lunged forward, jerking the leash from her hand and dashing toward the entrance. She took a few halting steps after the dog and Kix felt like his heart was going to explode with the fear of losing her.

His heart was still pounding furiously even after she'd taken cover behind her truck. He jammed on the brakes and stopped next to her, barely aware of getting out of the car before pulling her roughly into his arms.

Cady buried her face aganist Kix's chest and let him hold her for a minute before pulling back and saying,

"Somebody fired a gun in the barn. I heard two shots go off."

From inside the barn came the sounds of furious barking. Kix moved away from Cady and retrieved a gun from the rental car. "Stay here while I check it out."

"I'll call 911."

Kix nodded and moved toward the barn.

Cady watched, her heart thundering in her ears, her throat clogged with fear. If something happened to him... By the time he got to the doorway, she'd shaken off her paralysis and scrambled for her cell phone.

Kix figured he'd find a body in the barn and he did.

Tiny Johnson was propped up against a bale of hay, a bullet through his skull and a gun in his hand.

Two shots. One into Tiny. One with the gun in Tiny's hand so he'd have gunpowder residue on his skin. Only trouble was, there wasn't any blood spatter on Tiny's hand.

It was an easy mistake to make. Same as it was an easy mistake to figure no one would look past the baggie of coke or the syringe when they found Danny Meyers' body.

What Kix hadn't quite figured on seeing was Cady's dog hovering over Andrew Barwig, barking and flashing his teeth like a police dog. Damned if it wasn't a beautiful sight.

Kix moved in, remembering the command that his deputy used with the department's dog and told Ranger to "*sitz*". When the dog complied, Kix ordered Barwig onto his stomach with his arms flat on the ground and above his head, then yelled to Cady, telling her it was under control and to call Ranger and put him in the truck.

A police siren sounded in the distance. "Looks like we've got company coming, Andy. Somehow I don't think they're going buy this little suicide scenario. Don't reckon you'd like to save us all some trouble by confessing…"

His comment was greeted by silence.

"No, not your style. You're the type that likes to lawyer up quick. But you might want to keep it in mind that the SFPD already has your buddy Luke in custody. He doesn't strike me as a man who's going to keep quiet."

A second siren had joined the first and both were getting close. Despite the grim scene in the barn, Kix's heart raced with anticipation. When he was younger he liked steer wrestling. These days he got a kick out of taking down the bad guys. But right now neither of them compared to the prospect of going after Cady and getting her to accept his apology, and then his marriage proposal. There was no way he was going to let her get away from him.

Chapter Twenty

Cady felt like she was riding the edge of an emotional storm by the time she parked the truck in front of her house. Having Kix suddenly show up, realizing that he must have been following her, then being so afraid when he went into the barn and so relieved when he came out had opened up a Pandora's box of doubt and heartache...and hope.

She wasn't sure she could handle talking to him right now. But the determined look on his face when he'd said, "I'll follow you home," along with the fact that he was already out of his rental car and heading her way pretty much ruled out the possibility of delaying this. She got out of her truck, embarrassed by the way she was shaking.

Kix felt as nervous as a rookie cop. Damn, a lifetime of happiness was riding on how he handled this.

He sucked in a deep breath and shored up his nerve, his heart expanding and contracting, just about bursting with the need to hold Cady in his arms. And when he saw the slight tremors racing through her, he couldn't hold back. He pulled her up against his body and ran his hand along her back while he rubbed his face in her soft curls.

It felt so good to be in his arms that Cady just stood there, soaking in his warmth until the shaking stopped. But then self-preservation kicked in and she pulled away.

She took Ranger's leash and gave him permission to jump out of the truck then turned and made her way into the house. The minute she let the dog loose, there was a snick and the feel of smooth, cold steel against her wrist.

Cady looked down at the handcuff and watched as Kix closed the other one on his own wrist. "A lot of men would look down and see shackles, little darlin', but I'm seeing insurance. Now, you can go quiet and easy, or we can turn this into a rodeo event and spectator sport, but either way, we're going to talk, and afterwards you're going to pack up your things and head to Texas."

The emotional storm she'd been battling rose with the force of a hurricane and tears formed in Cady's eyes. Kix pulled her into his arms again. "Don't do that, Cady darlin', please don't cry. Hear me out, then if you need to throw a punch, go ahead and do it. Just don't cry or walk away. Damn, Cady, I couldn't take that. I love you."

When Cady didn't say anything, his gut went tight and Kix swallowed hard. Damned if his heart couldn't make up its mind whether it was going to burst right open or just plain shut down.

"Say you'll forgive me, darlin'. I know I hurt you and I'm sorry. Sorrier than I have the words for. I was thinking with my heart and not my head. I didn't want you anywhere close to danger."

Cady closed her eyes and rested her head against his chest, the erratic beat of his heart offering testimony to the fact he was on the same emotional roller coaster that she was on.

She believed him. Believing him was the easy part. She could even work up a joke about how not putting the little woman's life in danger was probably written in the Code of the West or something. But that didn't mean it hadn't really hurt.

She took a deep shuddering breath and lifted her face, looking into his worried eyes and seeing the vulnerability, seeing the desperate need to have his apology accepted and to get another chance.

No regrets. From the very start she'd made that promise to herself when it came to Kix. And right now, the only thing she'd ever regret would be throwing away a chance of a lifetime by letting hurt and pride get in the way of love.

She loved him. Wholeheartedly. Completely. Like she couldn't imagine loving another man. He was everything she'd ever wanted…and then some.

But maybe a little bit of caution was called for. He had to know that, cowboy code or not, she wanted his full acceptance of who she was and what some of her work involved.

"I'm okay now. I'm not mad. And I'd like to keep seeing you. Most of the Crime Tells cases I work are pretty tame, but there's still a chance one of them will go sideways. You have to accept that going in, Kix, and not try to protect me by keeping information from me."

Joy rushed through Kix at the acknowledgement that she was contemplating a future with him. "I trust you, darlin'. You're smart and capable. And besides that, you've got me and Ranger for backup."

Cady rubbed her cheek against his shirt, a ball of conflicting emotion in her chest. "So you meant it? You want me to stay with you in Texas for awhile?"

Kix pulled back so he could see her face. "For a lifetime, Cady. I want you to marry me." Then before she could start worrying about leaving her family, he added, "There's a Gulfstream jet and a pilot standing by at the

Kicking A Ranch. As long as you spend most of your nights in our bed, you can fly back and forth as much as you need to."

Cady's eyebrows went up. "That must be some ranching operation."

Kix grinned and brushed a kiss across her lips. "You'll love the Kicking A Ranch. It's home to fine horses, fine cattle, fine men and some mighty fine oil wells. Now put me out of my misery, Cady darlin' and tell me you'll marry me."

"What if I tell you I love you *and* I'll marry you?" She went to put her arms around his neck, but the handcuffs interfered. "And that maybe you'd better take these off."

"For now, darlin'. But I think we might just find a use for them in the bedroom."

Enjoy this excerpt from
Calista's Men
© Copyright Jory Strong, 2005

All Rights Reserved, Ellora's Cave Publishing, Inc.

Dante met his brother's gaze. Whatever was happening with Benito, he wanted it out on the table. "You've met someone?"

Benito's dark eyes, mirror images of his own, actually flashed with amusement momentarily, and then with surprise as his attention shifted to the bar entrance. "Not yet, but I'd like to."

Dante turned in his seat and his cock went from mildly interested to flat-out desperate, while at the same time his mind traveled from *oh yeah* at the sight of the dark-haired beauty to *oh fuck* when he saw who she came in with. "Shit."

The two women could almost be twins themselves except the one with the raven-black curls halfway down her back was just a little taller and oozed sensuousness while the one with the straight hair, the one who had Dante's cock pressing hard against his jeans, had an innocence about her that usually would have been more effective than a cold shower.

"You know her?" Benito asked, his cock thick and hard and straight as it strained to get past his waistband. He hadn't been with a women since the last one he and Dante had taken together, hadn't thought to seek one out either alone or with his brother — not that the need wasn't there, but it had changed and deepened until he knew a parade of easy, forgettable women wouldn't give him what he craved.

He hadn't intended to pursue a woman tonight. He hadn't even planned on bringing up the subject of women again until this mess with the shooting was over. He'd planned only on trying to persuade his brother to take over part of the Giancotti Security operation.

His intentions changed the moment the dark-haired woman walked into the bar and his heart tripped into an unsteady beat while his cock rose to rigid attention. He couldn't make out her features clearly, but she looked delicate, soft, with gentle curves that made him think of intense sex—followed by a lingering warmth instead of the usual need to disentangle and distance himself. "You know her?" Benito repeated, his eyes moving to Dante and seeing the lust riding his twin.

"The one with the long curls is Lyric Montgomery. Now Burke. She's married to a vice cop."

Benito gave a slight shake of his head confirming what Dante already knew. It was the woman with Lyric who had caught his brother's attention. "What about the other one?"

"I don't think I've seen her before." He shrugged. "But I don't spend a lot of time down here."

They watched as the two women found a table, then frowned identical frowns when a blond man sporting a ponytail just as long as Benito's joined them, receiving a hug and a kiss from both women before he sat down.

"I want to meet her," Benito said, hating the timing, hating that he had to push now when he'd been prepared to hold until Dante's head got clear about his career, hating that he risked opening a rift between them. But his gut, hell, his cock was screaming at him not to let the opportunity to meet this woman pass.

Dante gritted his teeth. Shit. Either way he was screwed. Benito would go over and introduce himself whether he went or not. "She's not what you usually go for," he said, already knowing it didn't matter. Hell, his own cock was aching for a chance at her.

Benito shrugged and rose from his seat. Cursing, Dante also stood.

Calista watched as the two men approached. God, they were gorgeous. Brothers, maybe twins, not identical, but close enough. She recognized the one with the shorter hair, his face had been in the news lately. He might be a cop, but he had the dark Italian looks and confidence of a street-wise gangster. Dante something. She should remember it. He'd been a topic of conversation around her parents' dinner table. To a one, the men in her family agreed he'd done what a cop had to do and made a righteous kill. Too bad the perp had come from a moneyed, politically inclined family.

She shivered—the pictures hadn't done Dante justice. The man was a walking orgasm, a sexual animal that could give a woman a night she'd never forget. Or repeat. His hard eyes and hard face were warning enough. The only thing he was offering was his body, and only while it suited him.

Calista's eyes moved to the brother and a ball of heated anticipation settled low in her belly, sending a warm flush through her cunt. She'd always had a thing for men with long hair, and this one, with the soft eyes and the lips that promised unspeakable pleasure, had her praying they weren't zeroing in on Lyric. That would be a major bummer. Not that she wouldn't understand it, but...

She straightened her shoulders. This was her night, and if a couple of guys couldn't resist hitting on Lyric, then she was not going to get upset about it. She wasn't going to let it ruin her excitement about getting a chance to work a case for Crime Tells. She was not in a competition with Lyric. Any guy would want to do her sister-in-law.

Of course, if they were stupid enough to try it, Kieran would convince them it wasn't a good idea. But...

"Oh shit," Lyric muttered, "Kieran is never going to believe I didn't have something to do with this."

"Not with your reputation," Tyler Keane agreed and Calista's attention shifted back to her companions.

"What?" she asked, her interest instantly piqued by the mischief dancing in Lyric's eyes. What had she ever done without Lyric in her life? Her sister-in-law was a walking catalyst for change.

"That's Dante Giancotti heading our way. I met him when I was helping Cady on her last case, well the last one before she took off to Texas with Kix." Lyric grinned. "Kieran was with me and I teased him with the prospect of introducing Dante to you."

Heat rushed to Calista's cheeks. She could just imagine how that had gone over. The men in her family tended to be overprotective, and that was a gross understatement. Calista shook her head. "Don't bother repeating what Big Brother said. I can guess."

Lyric actually snickered. "I won't have to. I'm sure he'll tell you himself when he gets here." Her eyes moved from the approaching Giancotti brothers to the exquisitely, delicious Tyler who'd been her childhood friend and who now worked as a police artist and as a consultant for Crime Tells. "But don't expect Kieran and I to stick around for long. Not with all this gorgeous male flesh present." Her eyebrows went up and down. "You know how your brother gets when he's around too much testosterone."

Calista was still laughing as Dante and his brother reached the table.

"Mind if we join you?" Benito asked after his brother and Lyric had made the introductions.

Lyric's laugh was pure mischief. "That'd be great, pull up a chair. We're celebrating. As of today, Calista is working for Crime Tells."

About the author:

Jory has been writing since childhood and has never outgrown being a daydreamer. When she's not hunched over her computer, lost in the muse and conjuring up new heroes and heroines, she can usually be found reading, riding her horses, or hiking with her dogs.

Jory welcomes mail from readers. You can write to her c/o Ellora's Cave Publishing at 1056 Home Avenue, Akron OH 44310-3502.

Why an electronic book?

We live in the Information Age—an exciting time in the history of human civilization in which technology rules supreme and continues to progress in leaps and bounds every minute of every hour of every day. For a multitude of reasons, more and more avid literary fans are opting to purchase e-books instead of paperbacks. The question to those not yet initiated to the world of electronic reading is simply: *why?*

1. *Price.* An electronic title at Ellora's Cave Publishing and Cerridwen Press runs anywhere from 40-75% less than the cover price of the <u>exact same title</u> in paperback format. Why? Cold mathematics. It is less expensive to publish an e-book than it is to publish a paperback, so the savings are passed along to the consumer.

2. *Space.* Running out of room to house your paperback books? That is one worry you will never have with electronic novels. For a low one-time cost, you can purchase a handheld computer designed specifically for e-reading purposes. Many e-readers are larger than the average handheld, giving you plenty of screen room. Better yet, hundreds of titles can be stored within your new library—a single microchip. (Please note that Ellora's Cave and Cerridwen Press does not endorse any specific brands. You can check our website at www.ellorascave.com or

www.cerridwenpress.com for customer recommendations we make available to new consumers.)

3. *Mobility.* Because your new library now consists of only a microchip, your entire cache of books can be taken with you wherever you go.

4. *Personal preferences are accounted for.* Are the words you are currently reading too small? Too large? Too...**ANNOYING**? Paperback books cannot be modified according to personal preferences, but e-books can.

5. *Instant gratification.* Is it the middle of the night and all the bookstores are closed? Are you tired of waiting days—sometimes weeks—for online and offline bookstores to ship the novels you bought? Ellora's Cave Publishing sells instantaneous downloads 24 hours a day, 7 days a week, 365 days a year. Our e-book delivery system is 100% automated, meaning your order is filled as soon as you pay for it.

Those are a few of the top reasons why electronic novels are displacing paperbacks for many an avid reader. As always, Ellora's Cave and Cerridwen Press welcomes your questions and comments. We invite you to email us at service@ellorascave.com, service@cerridwenpress.com or write to us directly at: 1056 Home Ave. Akron OH 44310-3502.

NEED A MORE EXCITING
WAY TO PLAN YOUR DAY?

ELLORA'S
CAVEMEN
2006 CALENDAR

COMING THIS FALL

THE
ELLORA'S CAVE
LIBRARY

Stay up to date with Ellora's Cave Titles
in Print with our Quarterly Catalog.

TO RECIEVE A CATALOG,
SEND AN EMAIL WITH YOUR NAME
AND MAILING ADDRESS TO:

CATALOG@ELLORASCAVE.COM

OR SEND A LETTER OR POSTCARD
WITH YOUR MAILING ADDRESS TO:
CATALOG REQUEST
c/o ELLORA'S CAVE PUBLISHING, INC.
1337 COMMERCE DRIVE #13
STOW, OH 44224

COMING TO A BOOKSTORE NEAR YOU!

ELLORA'S CAVE
2005

BEST SELLING AUTHORS TOUR

Discover for yourself why readers can't get enough of the multiple award-winning publisher Ellora's Cave. Whether you prefer e-books or paperbacks, be sure to visit EC on the web at www.ellorascave.com for an erotic reading experience that will leave you breathless.

www.ellorascave.com